G000113454

Foreign

To Christine — with memories of Hastings
Love Greg

Foreign
Correspondence

Gregory Andrusz

Matador
9 Priory Business Park,
Wistow Road, Kibworth Beauchamp,
Leicestershire. LE8 0RX
Tel: 0116 279 2299
Email: books@troubador.co.uk
Web: www.troubador.co.uk/matador
Twitter: @matadorbooks

ISBN 978 1788036 993

British Library Cataloguing in Publication Data.
A catalogue record for this book is available from the British Library.

Printed and bound by CPI Group (UK) Ltd, Croydon, CR0 4YY
Typeset in 11pt Aldine401 BT by Troubador Publishing Ltd, Leicester, UK

Matador is an imprint of Troubador Publishing Ltd

MIX
Paper from
responsible sources
FSC
www.fsc.org
FSC® C013604

For Ulybka

Contents

1

J C B

A few years ago, when I had just turned seventy, I reverted to my original name, Jakob Karl Braunsteig. Despite everything that happened towards the end of my life, I am living out my final days in a small village snuggled into a steep-sided valley in Gloucestershire, where I recently established and endowed a small charity, The JB Foundation, which is dedicated to helping young single mothers pursue their musical ambitions.

My German father, an engineer by profession who worked for Siemens, was posted to England before the First World War to manage one of the company's major investments over here. An open-minded and sociable person, he came to love that aspect of the English way of life that was quirky, ironical and non-conformist. At some point, he became a Quaker and when he eventually retired moved to Coalbrookdale, one of the spiritual homes of the movement in Shropshire.

Although he'd spoken out openly against German

militarism, he and his German wife were interned soon after hostilities began in 1914. They were released after a group of well-placed establishment figures successfully petitioned the Home Office on their behalf. Photographs in the family album, mostly taken during holidays spent in the countryside in both England and Germany, show his wife to be a tall, large-boned woman with no excess flesh and wide hips, whose square face tapered into a narrow, dimpled chin. She fell seriously ill on Armistice Day while giving birth to my much older sister, Birgit; she never fully recovered and died two years later.

Notwithstanding his undeserved imprisonment, my father decided to stay in England, and a few years later remarried. My birth coincided with my strong-willed half-sister's decision to go and live in Baiersdorf, a small town on the Rhine-Main canal, a few kilometres from Erlangen in Bavaria where her mother's childless sister and parents owned a small engineering firm, one of whose major customers had been Siemens. My undramatic appearance in the world came just months after the election of the new German Chancellor, sardonically referred to in the family archive as 'the painter and decorator from Linz', which accelerated my father's decision to anglicise our names so that I became James Charles Brown. Writing now as an old man, I cannot help but reflect and chuckle at how, by a strange act of fate, my initials were to be the same as those of a highly successful digging machine, the JCB, in whose manufacturer my father held shares that were to form part of my inheritance. Being an engineer I am sure that he must have greatly admired the ingenuity of the inventor of this earth-moving technology. He was not of course to know that as a piece of excavating equipment it would be the prime agent in my nemesis.

My mother, Helena, had attended a Quaker school for girls in Yorkshire whose headmistress had spent a number of years in Germany, where she had become very friendly with a particular school teacher of more or less the same age. Years later, after securing her position in the school and gaining a good reputation, she invited her friend, Frau Gertraud, to come to England to teach music and German at her school. It was through her that my mother developed such a love of opera and German culture that by the time she left school she was proud to declare herself to be a dedicated Germanophile.

It was as a German speaker that, after the war, she found a job with the Reparations Commission which required her to spend time in Berlin. To cut her exciting story short, before the Commission was wound up she applied for a job advertised in *The Times* for a fluent German speaker to become personal assistant to the General Manager of a major German manufacturer based in Britain. And that is how she met my father. Because they sheltered under the same panoply of Quaker values, held very similar progressive attitudes to relationships between men and women, and were passionate concert goers, she agreed to marry him. All that I can say, as their son, is that they were devoted to one another and included me in their love, which she passed on to me in her mother's milk.

She was in almost every way the very opposite to my father's first wife. While the latter was physically substantial, yet timid and diffident in character, my diminutive, Piaf-like mother gave vociferous expression to her anti-establishment views, which had been sown in the cradle by her own radically minded suffragette mother. Unlike Emmeline and her daughter Christabel Pankhurst, both of whom believed that so great was the danger posed by what they called the 'German Peril' they could not afford to expend vital energy on women's suffrage, my mother aligned herself with Emmeline's more radical daughters, Sylvia and Adel, who remained committed pacifists and adamantly refused to share their mother's enthusiasm for the war and rejected her entrenched anti-German sentiment.

My half-sister resembled her mother in height and build and had the same straight fair hair and perfectly proportioned nose. But in character she was her mother's antithesis; rather than being shy and self-effacing, Birgit was strident and outward going so that it came as no surprise to my parents, or to the pupils in her old school, when we heard that she had joined the National Socialist Youth Movement and quickly risen in its structure.

For my part I had a small frame like my mother but had my father's long, thin-fingered hands, full lips and hooded, owlish eyes nestling under a widow's peak. From both of them I inherited a strong sense of justice and belief in pacifism, which was bolstered by the ethos of the nearby Quaker school to which they sent me as a boarder in September 1939, having months earlier recognised that war was inevitable.

I don't remember exactly who first shouted at me 'Charlie Brown, he's a clown', though I do know that I was still at primary school and the name stuck. Since my father had been born in Hamelin, a town made famous by the Grimm tale of the Pied Piper, he thought that an amusing way of attaching me to his German stump would be to give me a tin whistle which, as it happened, was a musical instrument perfectly matched to the name I had been given.

Looking back to those very early years, what can I say that I remember? It's me as a little boy strutting around the garden in a pair of Wellington boots, wearing my father's traditional feathered hat, playing my whistle as in the legend, diligently learning my scales on the piano, and listening to my mother sing, recite and read to me in German. This early experience was the foundation for my love of music and my ear for sounds and languages.

Naturally, when I went to secondary school I took the whistle with me. During one of our first music lessons the teacher asked if any of us played an instrument. Because of our social backgrounds, three of the other pupils did: Carolyne played the violin, William was a flamboyant horn player, who later became a florid interpreter of its canon, while Jocelyn had received tutoring in the piano as soon as he could read. After they had declared themselves, the teacher looked around the class, catching each of us in the eye.

'Who else can play?' he asked again. I hesitated for a moment then put up my hand and told them with a snicker about my musical talent. The teacher raised his arms to heaven and gave a broad smile, which served as a conductor's baton for the class to laugh. Although I hadn't really done that much to merit the nickname, this tiny episode in the first couple of weeks in my new school indelibilised my name and role.

Try as I might at different times to surreptitiously unpick the stitched-on label and dump it into the dustbin of my unwanted personal effects, someone always came along and pinned it back on again, so that in the end I accepted it and its associated persona. Over the years the role I had been allotted brought both deserved and undeserved rewards and penalties. In the end, though, I must leave it to you to decide whether that's what you would call me; whether my life justified the appendage to my name.

Academically, I was an average all-rounder but, unlike my father, had no aptitude at all for the natural sciences or their practical sibling, engineering. For his sake I made a big effort to pass my science examinations and learn enough about the workings of the combustion engine that I could undertake minor car repairs. Sports and music were the only parts of the curriculum where I demonstrated any flair, managing good times in long distance running and playing a good game of tennis. As for music, my teacher channelled my penchant for wind instruments away from the whistle to the clarinet.

Being taught in a mixed school and tutored by adults, some of whom did little to conceal their dalliances, was conducive to sexual precociousness. While boys who toyed with homo-eroticism remained forever liminal heterosexuals, only a few girls left the school wearing trousers and cropped hair. By the end of the third year I knew on which side of my body my sexual pleasure was buttered and by the time I went into the fifth form, Judith, who was a year ahead of me, and I were looked upon, in today's terminology, as an item. At the end of that summer term, after performing well in the school's sports day, Charlie Brown piped his first paramour into the long grass and pregnancy.

It was not the first occasion that the school secretary and her lover, the classics teacher, famous for introducing pupils to the lewder lines penned by Catullus – *pedicabo ego vos et irrumabo* and so on – had turned to their sexually progressive contacts in South London for advice. An abortion was arranged without fuss. Fortunately, however, Judith had a miscarriage during a strenuous hiking holiday in the Dolomites and returned to the sixth form to complete her examinations foetus free.

To the boys I was some sort of folk hero; to the girls I was living up to my name, while Judith was the teenage heroine. In retrospect I behaved badly throughout, but at the time I defended myself by entering in my personal social audit ledger a plea of 'confused teenager'. To say that I was 'scarred' by the episode would be far too dramatic and untrue; a better metaphor to describe the effect of the event is to see me as having been infected by a virus that would lie dormant inside me until, much later in life, a concatenation of circumstances would trigger an unexpected emotional reaction. At the time, as an act of contrition and in order to distract myself from those disquieting emotions, guilt and shame, which were harassing my body psychosomatically, I began to devote greater energy to my study of music and to practising the clarinet more diligently.

The following year, my last at the school, I competed with Carolyne for a school bursary to go to music college. I was pleased with the way I performed my chosen pieces by Carl Maria von Weber but, unfortunately for me, Carolyne was an exceptionally gifted violinist and won the award. The music teacher wrote to my parents telling them that, although the bursary had gone to someone else, under normal circumstances, because my recital had been 'outstanding' and I had 'exceeded expectations' in the written examination, funds would have been found from some source or other for me to continue my studies; however, the war had taken its toll on all such little pots of money. My parents were so delighted to hear such a commendation that they decided to pay the fees for me to attend one of the best music colleges in the country if I managed to pass the entrance examination.

The day after the postman brought the letter telling me that I had been accepted, I received my call-up papers for National Service, from which my Quaker background did not exempt me. However, following an exchange of correspondence with the Ministry of

Defence, I was offered a typically British solution that avoided confrontation over matters of principle: the Ministry allowed me to defer my enlistment until I had completed my studies; I would then join the Band of the Royal Air Force Regiment where I would be assigned duties associated with the regimental band and be spared military combat duties.

To my college tutors I was a diligent student who managed to demonstrate a good command of technique, a solid grasp of the theory of harmony and of the historical development of the Western musical tradition. My tin whistle as ever found me friends and, because of my involvement in all sorts of non-academic, extra-curricular college activities, I was christened an extrovert (in effect, a higher status clown) and though I had outgrown the gown of the clown and the name 'Charlie' I quickly became a 'Jimmy', though thankfully never 'Jimmy the Joker'.

I am sure that it was because of my team spirit that the tutors volunteered to give me that little bit extra of their time; however, I needed more than just a bit more tuition for, while I had some musical talent, no one believed I had the makings of a maestro. My school teacher and college tutors knew that, my father guessed it, my mother tried to deny it and by my second year at college I acknowledged it. My father, a practical and problem-solving man, convinced my mother that, if I were to earn a living as a musician, as it seemed I was set on doing, then someone would have to be found and paid to give me the additional instruction considered necessary.

Three people independently mentioned a former graduate, Kenneth. Ten years older than me, he already had a contract with a chamber orchestra and played in a quartet, but the income from these sources was barely enough for him to pay his way. Such is the randomness of life: while I had been endowed with limited musical talent and was already a pledged sensualist, whose attitudes and tastes had been nurtured by my financially secure family, Ken was musically gifted and a well-read autodidact but materially impoverished.

A combination of both his talent as a teacher and his perseverance, a character trait bred and fed by circumstances, enabled me to achieve distinctions in some of my examinations. But, since in the world of music passing examinations does not ensure employment, his tutoring role involved taking me to a wide variety of concert venues – jazz and dance as well as classical – to watch and be introduced to experienced musicians. All our expenses were covered by my parents, to whom he had endeared himself for having encouraged me to explore ways to exploit two of my major social assets – my bilinguality and having a half-sister in Germany.

By the time I reached my final examination, I had set my distant goal to become second clarinettist in an established orchestra. It has always seemed to me that one should aim high but never too high for, to

borrow from Mr Micawber: to aim too high and fail
– result, agonising abomination; aim to a point above
the mediocre and succeed beyond expectation – result,
boundless satisfaction. According to my college director
of studies, who was not much older than me and with
whom I socialised outside college, my chances of
achieving even this limited aim would be improved if
I pursued my studies further. And so I decided that as
soon as I had completed my deferred National Service I
would go to Germany to continue my education.

Not long after I had started my air force training,
opportunities arose for me to be stationed abroad,
including in Germany. Although I found the idea of
travelling very attractive and considered that there was a
good chance that I could benefit from the experience of a
tour of duty in Germany, my parents deemed it prudent
for me not to apply for a posting, advising me to keep a
low profile about my German parentage and knowledge
of the language. In their view, any benefits that I might
gain from a successful application would be outweighed
by the fact that I would be required to reveal more details
about my background, which would expose me to the
prejudices embedded in the military establishment and
worse still to the bigotry and anti-German sentiments of
some of the men, especially regulars and NCOs, with
whom I would be living and training. My mother, whose
ear was well attuned to the Cold War times, speculated

that it was quite conceivable that I might be invited to join the intelligence service, which we were sure already knew about my father's original nationality and possibly his family connections. She was adamant that I should steer well clear of any temptation to go down that path, pointing out that whether I accepted or rejected any proposal that they might make to me, I would be compromised for the rest of my life.

The fact that I never actually bothered to probe my parents on the reasons for their concern over this issue could be put down to my having internalised some of their anxiety. By this date I knew that my father, even though he had anglicised his name and been naturalised, felt himself to be an alien and, as I learned later, was sometimes treated as such on the familiar grounds that a leopard never changes its spots and all that. My pedigree English mother empathised with her husband, while I, the English born and educated son, suppressed any such empathetic feeling.

But, it was not just this particular issue that I did not probe; generally speaking, it was extremely rare for me to question my parents' judgements or contradict their opinions on anything. I am a little ashamed to say it, but no one could have been more conventional and less rebellious and less of a contrarian than me. On the other hand, I like to think that I compensated for being acquiescent by cultivating an image of myself as a fun-seeking person, which way into my adult years meant being quite willing to take part in, or even be the instigator of, the odd practical joke.

Because I had the facility for playing the fool as well as a musical instrument, I was accepted for what I was and so was never nastily bullied or required to go out on weekend benders. I had an additional advantage over the others in my regiment: I was accustomed to institutional life. Taken together my two years of compulsory service to the State passed uneventfully. In truth, I was no more than a clerk in military uniform who worked in the section that dispatched food and clothing by air to regions still badly affected by the wartime destruction and disruption. I left the Services that much older and only a little more worldly wise.

The limited postal contact that existed between my father and Birgit, my sister, in the early days after she had gone to live in Germany ceased altogether in 1938 when he had invited her to come back to England for a holiday. His last letter sent to her in June 1939 was returned unopened. On the basis that she might still be living at her pre-war address in Baiersdorf, I found out more about two old and distinguished universities in the region, about 50 kilometres from one another: Bamberg and Erlangen. In the end I registered for the following academic year at Bamberg and with a generous financial contribution from my father together with a few names and addresses, I booked a passage on a cargo boat from Harwich to Bremerhaven with the intention of taking a boat along the Weser to Hamelin to satisfy my curiosity about my father's birthplace before travelling on to Baiersdorf.

When I disembarked, milling around on the quayside was a small group of British soldiers, whom I nervously approached, and not knowing how they might respond to me asked if they knew how I might cadge a berth on a barge. During the course of a bantering exchange, I told them that I played the clarinet; it did not take much effort on their part to persuade me to postpone my journey southward for a few days.

Ten weeks later, after a few performances at their military base followed by several engagements at clubs and other places, someone I had got to know wangled a place for me on a long, narrow freighter going upstream. Early one morning, armed with a pre-war, leather-bound Baedeker guide to Lower Saxony, Hessen and Bavaria purchased from a market bookstall, I jumped down on to the barge and I was on my way again.

The unexpected short diversion had been worthwhile; it gave me time to find my feet, adjust to being a citizen from an occupying power (while at the same time being half-German), earn some money, gain experience of playing in front of an audience, brush up my colloquial German and learn first-hand about the situation in the country. Although much of my information about the society reflected the perceptions of the victors, it was rounded out by what I saw and heard during my cycle rides through the surrounding countryside.

It was only when I told my military hosts that

Hamelin was to be my first stop that I learned that for them the town's notoriety came not from its being the home of the legendary rat-catcher but from its prison, which after the war had been used by the British as a detention centre for German war criminals. Batting away their googlies about my interest in visiting the town was not difficult; at the same time its recent history and association with 'the Great Escape' from Stalag Luft III in 1944, of which by now I had vaguely heard, gave added reason for stopping there.

I only stayed for a day – long enough to see the house in which my father had been born, catch a bus to the Klütturm, the sightseeing tower just outside Hamelin with its panoramic view of the town, and send a postcard of the prison to my father asking rhetorically what he knew about it. The following morning I was back on the same barge and on my way down to Münden where the Weser is formed from the confluence of the Fulda and Werra rivers.

Having unloaded part of its cargo and taken on new freight, the boat continued down the river Fulda, leaving me to stretch my legs around the town, much of whose historical centre – with its medieval town hall, its white-painted houses with their contrasting coal-black half-timber frames, some with high gables and carved wood façades – had hardly been damaged at all during the war. That same evening I caught the train to Bamberg, my destination, sharing my compartment with one other silent fellow traveller.

The person with whom I shared a father had for years been struggling to crawl from my unconscious and push herself into the dullish light of my daily existence. During my school years she had been stubbornly buried; my birth country was at war with Germany, where she had chosen to live. Two particular older pupils, who liked to push and elbow me in the corridor and hiss 'Hun' when they passed, once sardonically quizzed me about my father's accent. I explained it away by saying that, though English, his mother was Norwegian and so he had spent his early years and much of his school holidays in Norway until he started work. It was not until Ken had talked openly with me about my sister that she began her journey through to my consciousness to become real and come alive. Now I was on my way to the small town between Bamberg and Erlangen where she had gone to live over twenty years ago.

When I climbed down off the train at Baiersdorf I was pleasantly surprised to find the single-platform station brightly decorated with window boxes and tubs of flowers. In response to my enquiry of where I could find accommodation, a man wearing a peaked cap and dressed in a station master's uniform, the fabric shiny through wear and frequent ironing, directed me to the 'Gasthof Adler' two streets away, where I was offered a room for only three days because after that all the rooms were taken for a fortnight. I signed myself in as

James Brown and went to my clean, sparsely furnished room, unpacked and went down for a supper of beer, cured boar meat, sauerkraut and pumpernickel. When I had finished I ordered a coffee and enquired after the Mühlrad family, my father's in-laws.

'Herr and Frau Mühlrad both died a few years ago. Their daughter, Ingrid, runs the factory now and is doing a good job of building the business up again,' he answered.

'Does she run it all by herself?' I asked.

He shrugged his shoulders and puckered his lips signalling a reluctance to enter into conversation, but nonetheless added, 'Her niece, who was born in England and lived here before the war, has just come back from somewhere or other and we expect that she'll take over the main management.'

I did not read the landlord's taciturnity as hostility to foreigners, but as the visage of a misanthrope who lacked the propensity for small talk and only engaged with people because, as the owner of a small hotel, he felt vaguely obliged to do so. Rightly or wrongly, I decided that any further questioning on my part would be unwelcome.

The next morning I walked to the factory on the eastern outskirts of the town, about a mile from the Adler, accompanied by a small rucksack of jostling, disjointed and confused emotions. Remember, I was a young – not very adult – twenty-two year old, not that worldly, and suddenly unsure of my identity and standing in the country where my father had been born and in whose soil I had shallow roots, or so it seemed to me at the time.

I walked through a wide iron gate set into a three-metre-high brick wall and into a yard, where two motor engines, partially covered with tarpaulin, sat on the floor of a small truck. Behind this loading area were three long, single-storey buildings – the manufacturing workshops. A heavy glass door at the end of the nearest of them protected the entrance to an office. I pushed the door open and went through. As I approached the counter, a middle-aged woman came out of another door. Dressed in a dirndl, her thick hair swept back from the forehead and knotted into a bun, stood the person whom I instinctively took to be my father's sister-in-law.

'Guten Tag,' she greeted. 'Which company are you from?'

'I am not from any company. My name's James Brown. I am the son of Hermann Braunsteig,' I said. The vacuum between us was filled with a wholly natural silence. It could scarcely have been otherwise, for how was she to react to such an out-of-the-blue announcement? With joy at the appearance of a long-lost nephew? Hardly. Why should she?

The creased forehead and wrinkled eyes that would be normal for anyone her age were etched deeper by the ferocious internecine war from which her nation – not just the Government – had emerged defeated. We remained in a static stillness for a few moments, then she began to nod her head slowly and sway her shoulders gently; her lips gradually parted, her eyebrows buckled upwards until her face was transformed into a smile.

'Well, well. I am Ingrid Mühlrad, your sister's aunt. We're expecting Birgit back tonight.' She paused then asked, 'When did you arrive here? And where are you staying?'

'Yesterday. At the Adler.'

'Pack your things and come over to the house. Before Birgit arrives you can meet your nieces and nephew; I suppose that's what they are.'

I returned to the Gasthof, told the landlord that I was going to stay with Frau Mühlrad, and that she was my aunt. I pronounced her status with some pride. He narrowed his eyes slightly, looked me up and down, something he had not done when I first arrived, waggled the turnip on his shoulders and said, 'You must be Birgit's English brother.'

'Yes. I am,' I answered in a self-important voice.

'I can't say you look much like her, but there we are. I don't look much like my sister either.' He bent and wrote out the bill. I paid, shook hands and left.

My aunt came out of the office as I walked through the factory gate. In the courtyard, a pre-war Mercedes-Benz had taken the place of the truck. Its driver drove us along a small road directly south from the factory into a less densely populated district and after a mile or so we came to a group of substantial, detached two- and three-storey mansarded houses, each set in its own large garden with mature hardwood trees and orchard. The buildings exuded a bourgeois solidity that no doubt matched the conservatism of their residents. The wealth accumulated by their owners in the good times had been well invested and the war had taken little toll. Once they had dealt with the odd slipped roof tile, unhinged shutter and rusted railings, little else would have to be done to return the houses to their previous standard and the residents to the social status that they'd enjoyed until towards the end of our most recent pan-European fratricidal conflict.

As soon as we were in the car she began to talk. 'Birgit has three children. Ilse, the youngest, is ten, Konrad is twelve and Eva can't be that much younger than you. I've been trying to work it out. Birgit came here in 1933 when she was fifteen. And, that's the year you were born, isn't it?'

'Yes. I was born in 1933.' Her physical presence was so dominant that I could only confirm what she had said; she had asked a straightforward question and only wanted corroboration not elaboration.

'Simple arithmetic makes you twenty-two. And Eva's a grown-up sixteen year old.'

I stayed with my new family in Baiersdorf for two months, leaving at the beginning of October to meet my tutor in Bamberg. As soon as I had settled into my digs I turned my scattered notes and fresh memories of the time I had spent with my sister and her family into a detailed *aide-mémoire*. What I am going to recount now is a fragment of my written record, giving the bare bones of my sister's history. By way of summary, when I met her in 1955, Birgit still expressed herself as a German patriot who was furious that what had begun as a vision of a revival of the German people had gone so badly wrong.

'I can tell you, James, that when I was at school in England, sometimes being German was not funny,' she started by saying. 'They couldn't physically bully me. I was too tough for that. Instead I was often cold-shouldered. Of course, not everyone had it in for me. No, I did have friends, some good ones, and we kept in touch after I left. One of the things which upset me was that Papa did not go to the school and complain about the way I was being treated. I know he wanted to keep a low profile and to be accepted by the English, but all the same. On top of that he was obsessed with the new woman in his life, your mother, which only made me feel worse than ever about being in England.'

Here were the roots of her conservatism and nationalism; she had lost her mother, something which she did not want to talk about, felt betrayed by her father and was ostracised at school. With the hindsight of being a father myself I would just add as a postscript that these specific grievances were kneaded into and intensified the feelings of melancholy and disaffection frequently experienced by adolescents. In contrast to the cumulative sense of rejection in England, she had been warmly welcomed by her grandparents and aunt whose firm's fortunes were steadily reviving. Healthy and sporty, rather like me, she joined the youth movement, of which she became an enthusiastic member, attending their summer camps, going winter skiing and mountaineering, and actively recruiting other young people.

'You know,' she had said, 'a lot of people thought that the policies advocated by the NSDAP were just what Germany needed at the time. And it was not solely about dealing with unemployment and inflation. Many Germans, even some of those who were persecuted and very badly treated by the Government, wanted the national socialist movement to succeed. Like us, they believed that there was no other alternative to dealing with the chaos the country was in. I can tell you the movement's idealism, strictness and patriotism were highly attractive. We liked the fact that the Party didn't look back nostalgically to a pre-industrial past but forward to a technologically driven future. As far as I was aware at the time, most of the Party's supporters did not agree with the violence perpetrated by thugs and gangsters on our streets. But they were all manifestations of the total disorder and lawlessness of the time. We were on the verge of civil war. And there was something else that you should know: the movement was not just about us Germans and our particular domestic problems. Germany was the cultural heart of Europe and we wanted that fact to be recognised by other countries. And, James, like it or not, believe you me the time will come when Germany will once again be the continent's cultural heart. The war was, if you pardon the expression, a bloody setback. Anyway, you can put all that to one side in order to grasp our real mission. Do you know what that was?' Birgit stared me in the eye demanding a response.

'To provide Germans with *Lebensraum*?' I ventured with a grimace.

'Nein! It was to deliver Europe from Bolshevism. Even your very own Mr Churchill, when he was Secretary of State for War during the First World War, declared that the West would rue the day it failed to suffocate the baboon of Bolshevism in its cradle. You've probably never heard that quotation before, but those were his words: 'the baboon of Bolshevism'. Then, he changed his mind and left it to us to take on the Bolsheviks, but instead of leaving us to get on with the job, he stabbed us in the back by attacking us in Africa and Italy.

'Looking back,' Birgit continued, 'I still see nothing wrong with what the Party initially set out to do. It just went wrong; very badly wrong as far as ordinary Germans are concerned. The whole thing became distorted by idiots and fanatics, leaving us Germans as the scapegoats for the mess that we are all in today. I take consolation from the thought that in the next fifty years another group of fanatics will have a good attempt at harnessing the *Zeitgeist* for their purposes and so take the eyes of Europe off us.'

'James does not want a history lesson, Birgit,' Ingrid intervened. 'He'll learn about the war and what led to it from a different perspective while he's with us and with other people he'll be mixing with. Tell him a bit about the family.'

'Alright. I met Gerhardt Bruckmeier, who was a young professional officer, in the summer of 1938 in Bamberg. It was my first ball. The following twelve months were the happiest of my life; the fact that war was in the air gave an added frisson to everything we did. Since Gerhardt had to join the Party, I did too; we had an officers' wedding and Eva was born. Gerhardt fought on the Western front, was decorated and promoted. He was posted to three more combat zones where, having served with distinction, he was again promoted in rank and as a reward in 1942 was given an administrative role in Breslau, where Konrad and Ilse were born. We lived very comfortably in a peaceful, untroubled environment and made the very most of all the cultural pursuits and social pastimes that were on offer. Our papa, yours and mine, loved opera and so did we. We never missed a single performance of a new production in Breslau or Dresden.'

We all sat quietly listening to her reminiscences. She came to an end, smiled at us, breathed in deeply and with a watering eye let out a muffled whimpering groan.

'Our world simply collapsed. January 1945 became our Götterdämmerung as a family and as a country. On 26 January, the day after Gerhardt's birthday, we started to make our preparations to leave the city. Gerhardt provided us with a car and driver and I left with Eva, two-year-old Konrad and nine-month-old Ilse. It was freezing, but Gerhardt had been right. Two weeks after we left, Breslau's remaining rail connection westward was cut off by the Soviet encirclement. Initially we took the main road towards Görlitz and Dresden, but this was so crowded that, despite our privileged and protected status, our driver decided that it would be safer to go south on a small road towards Schweidnitz which, incidentally, is no longer German. Luckily, he knew the whole area like the back of his hand having chauffeured senior civilian and military officials to the region's numerous health spas, ski resorts and hunting lodges from before the war. He navigated a clever detour through the mountains to Schreiberhau and from there we made our way to Karlsbad where we knew people and stayed for over a week to recuperate. Don't forget I was still breastfeeding! That beautiful spa now belongs to the Czechs. So much for the Sudetenland! It took another three days to reach Baiersdorf.'

'Why didn't you take the train to Dresden? Wouldn't it have been the quickest way of getting back here?' I asked, hoping to demonstrate that I was listening attentively, not that I could recognise the route she had taken without looking at a map.

'Didn't you ever hear or read about what Churchill did to that beautiful city?' she asked sardonically, leaning back in her chair. She looked at her aunt and each of the children and, moving her eyes from face to face, spoke about her husband. I didn't know whether this was the first time her children had heard the story or whether it was a recital they had listened to a hundred times.

'As a colonel, Gerhardt, your papa,' she said nodding to each of her children in turn, 'who was your step-brother-in-law, James,' wagging a finger at me, 'was put in charge of forming fighting units in Breslau out of a hotchpotch of young people and anyone else who could be pulled in as reserves. It was a mess! I heard later that, despite the overwhelming odds against us, even as late as March we managed to drive the Bolsheviks back. The scale was different, but in terms of sheer brutality, Breslau can be compared with Stalingrad; if international conventions counted for virtually nothing on the Eastern front, then during those last days of the defence of Breslau they counted for nothing at all.'

I do not really know why I intervened but I did. The catalyst was almost certainly the alcohol I had been drinking; I only drank at mealtimes and then only the odd glass of beer or wine, so by this point I was most definitely tiddly. Nonetheless, the wine was really just the taper to the fury building up in me and forcing me to somehow tell Birgit that her narrative was flawed, for Germany had been the aggressor. But because it was not in my nature to say anything so direct, my reply to her account of events was characteristically oblique.

'I was educated in a Quaker school from the age of six,' I said in a slightly cocky and conceited way. 'Quaker!' Birgit exclaimed. The reactive moment, encapsulated in her expressed amazement, passed and she took in air to reflect on my bizarre upbringing that she was only now learning about. While she pondered, I continued:

'History had an important place in our school

curriculum, but the history that we were taught was quite different from that in other schools. Firstly it did not glorify England's past. Secondly, our teachers convinced us that all wars are bad; whatever reasons may be invoked to justify them, wars mean enemies and enemies legitimise the latent maliciousness found lurking in most human beings. And, once we reach the point where we see, or we're told that we're surrounded by, enemies then in no time we're on the slippery slope to becoming dehumanised, a condition that allows us to condone all sorts of brutal behaviour. What I know about what happened in Stalingrad and what you're now telling me about Breslau were predictable outcomes of war.'

Birgit shook her head. I had missed the point. She did not want to hear about historical parallels. She wanted me to listen to the eulogy she was delivering about her husband and to what she had lost. She wanted me to understand her and him and her side of the family from their point of view not from the position of a member of the victor's family. She cocked her head to one side and slid her hand across the table towards me and said slowly and not at all harshly, 'If you can park your Quaker ideals and drink when it's convenient, you're capable of doing the same and… kill.' She pulled her hand back and twiddled her wedding ring and continued:

'After an eighty-day siege, Breslau was our last *Festung* to fall. I don't know whether you do or don't know but Berlin surrendered to the Soviets on 2 May. Hamburg did the same to the British on 3 May. By now all the capitals in Europe were controlled by the Allies, except Prague. Anyway the garrison there couldn't help us. Still, we held out until 6 May.' She paused then, looking at her aunt, said, 'My husband was given the option, which he refused, to join General Niehoff and the fanatical Gauleiter, Karl Hanke, in – guess where – the basement of the university library. Hanke of all people! In case you've forgotten, let me remind you that in his final testament Hitler named Hanke the successor to Himmler as Reichsführer-SS. Think about it.'

After this torrent of emotion and history, my mouth dropped open and the only question that I could ask was, 'What happened to Hanke?'

I have only seen once since then such anger in anyone's face and the vehemence with which Birgit answered made me flinch. 'That man was the most despicable in the whole Reich. On the day before the surrender, after raging about betrayal then declining the suggestion from General Niehoff that he commit suicide, he escaped by plane to the Sudetenland, or so we're told. But no one knows his real fate; there are different stories: some say that he made it to South America; others that he was caught and killed by Czech partisans, and there's one account that he had a bullet in the head from a drunk against whom he was characteristically railing. Anyway, I don't care a shit what happened to that bastard. Excuse me. I am sorry I swore.' She shook her head and changed into a more placatory gear as she turned onto ground that she obviously liked to coast across. 'You know, I don't believe that Gerhardt died during those final battles; no, I think that, despite the so-called honourable conditions secured by Niehoff, he was one of those put in cattle trucks to fill Stalin's gulag. So, he might still be alive.'

I then made a very stupid remark: 'Birgit, European history is full of examples of situations where defenders, who capitulated under the understanding that they would be spared, were butchered the moment they laid down their arms.' I had said my piece, shut up and waited.

Birgit's hands were cupped around her wine glass. Her eyes glazed over momentarily then holding the stem she lifted it and held it out towards me and said with a grin, 'Prost, James!' We clinked the tilted rims of crystal and took a final goodnight sip.

My *aide-mémoire* ended with the reflexive thought that has been my lodestar ever since: never ever draw historical comparisons when people are talking about the most momentous events in their own lives. They have no interest in empathising with the tragedy of anyone else, for that would detract from and diminish the exceptionality with which they regard their own misery and misfortune; it's no surprise that people bereaved by war are often amongst those who most resent pacifists.

★

During my two years at the music college, having extended my studies by a year, I regularly visited

Baiersdorf mainly, it has to be said, to see Eva. For me, as a young man, Birgit's daughter had the exotic attraction commonly found in someone from a different culture. Besides, I had seen her develop from being a gangly Nabokovesque, slightly awkward adolescent into a young woman who was physically striking, witty and a talented conversationalist. We were the natural stuff of each other's sexual fantasy, which was edging towards the precipice of bloody carnality. Whatever might have happened did not, because during my last visit to Baiersdorf, the week before my return to England for the summer, my sister snuffed the candle flame of lust when she found us kissing – an act, which according to the convention of the time amounted to being caught *in flagrante delicto*.

The effect was immediate: the temperature in the house fell and the mask of smiles was replaced by the turned-down lips of tragedy. So, when I caught the train home it was not just for a holiday; it was for the next twenty years. Still, I had established a family link. My father, not terribly expressive emotionally and never being told about the Eva episode, was cheered by my small achievement in re-establishing family contact, especially with his daughter. A few months later he went with my mother on what was for him a soulful journey to visit Birgit and his other relatives in Baiersdorf. (For reasons I never asked about he made no effort to try to find members of his own Braunsteig family.) Over the next quarter of a century, our families maintained only an intermittent exchange across the Channel.

★

My departure from Germany marked the end of my apprenticeship as a clarinettist and musician; with my arrival back in England I was about to enter into my journeyman stage. It was then that I felt that I was standing not so much at a crossroad as at a T-junction where I could choose either to take the path leading to a conventional career, or try something less orthodox; I still believe that being able to make such a choice is easier for a musician than it is for members of many other professions.

I grew a beard, joined a jazz band, fell in love with a staunch Bohemian called Angela, and we went to live on a canal barge. The company I kept looked upon music as a way to challenge the cultural and political hegemony of the bourgeoisie, as they used to say; Shostakovich's orchestrations and the experimental music of Schoenberg and Cage represented rebuffs to the hypocritical harmony of the status quo. I quickly learned how to identify and refute the fallacies of the soft anti-communist propaganda that I had received during my military service, and for a while agreed with my fellow travelling angry young men that the Soviet Union was the future.

Though I conformed in my dress, speech and behaviour to that of my adopted peer group, I often felt detached from them and more of a self-conscious observer of myself in their company than a member of it. This feeling contributed to my increasingly unpleasant arguments with Angela, which were no longer confined to the hours immediately after a bout of cider drinking. When, one day, she walked across the gangplank from our barge-home to live with an Italian anarchist, in order, in her words, 'to be truer to herself', that is precisely what I did too, for very soon afterwards I closed the door to my laboratory and turned my back on my short-lived experiment with the unconventional.

I moved around the country in search of work – as a member of an orchestra for a season or as a temporary teacher or private tutor – until I met Magda, who at the time was the deputy editor of a popular magazine. After a brief courtship we believed that we had sufficient in common plus that certain undefinable *je ne sais quoi* to invite a handful of our mutual and respective friends to join us at a London registry office for the official marriage ceremony and then for celebratory drinks in a rented functions room in a Soho watering hole. We informed our parents of our decision after the event.

Like most couples, our relationship in its very early stages had a symbiotic quality, but for most of the time it was parasitical; at first, during my journeyman stage, I drew sustenance from Magda, who had successfully climbed the editorial tree, moving in the space of a handful of years from deputy editor of a magazine with a miniscule circulation to being editor of a journal with an international readership. She travelled extensively at home and abroad fêting potential advertisers and contributors; she was a high earner and we dined well on her income.

After a while I thought it would be nice to start a family; she reflected on the issue for a further couple of years then, without telling me, had her coil removed. Julian and Ralph were born in quick succession, and that's when the tide turned and I became the principal earner. Soon after the birth of my younger son, I was given a contract with one of the principal English chamber orchestras and Magda retired to become the household manager, a role that she never found fulfilling.

Thus ended my journeyman phase and I became, in old-fashioned parlance, a 'master'. Phrased differently, I had entered the antechamber of the third age, and though I did not at all look like Giorgione's depiction of an old man in his painting *Le tre età dell'uomo*, I had most definitely acquired the bundle of standard accessories associated with this stage in the life-cycle: a wife, grown-up children, mortgaged home and regular income. Around about this time, I bumped into Angela of my barge and beard phase at a lunchtime jazz session in a riverside pub. After an amicable exchange, we agreed that we had both turned out to be true to ourselves; she was exactly the same as when I had first met her and my life was still extremely ordinary. Yet at the same time, despite my conventionality, lying dormant inside Jimmy Brown was good old Charlie Brown, always itching to play his tin whistle.

Orchestras that play classical music, like bands that play popular music, go on tours and both have their loyal followers, a few of whom need little formal courting to follow an instrumentalist from his music sheet to his bed sheet. It's a long time ago now, but I recall the occasion quite vividly. Our orchestra had been engaged to play a series of concerts in the north of England and at our third venue I felt sure that I recognised one petite, elfin-looking woman – young but certainly not a teenager – who had been present at the previous two concerts. Her face had registered with me simply because whenever I looked up from my music, it seemed that I invariably caught her eye.

I eventually met her at a post-performance reception in a city which, during its prime, had been a global leader in its manufacturing sector, but which had now transformed itself into a city known for its cultural vibrancy. She was talking, glass in hand, her foot tilted in a low-heeled shoe, towards Bertie, our jovial, larger than life manager. Beckoned by her demeanour, I went up to join them and he introduced me:

'Jimmy, this is Jenny. Jenny this is our Jimmy.' (My odd attempts to be a James had never succeeded and having resigned myself to being known by the familiar form of my name I had come to prefer it.)

'Jenny and Jimmy,' he continued, 'your names, at least those you're both known by, really suit you nicely.' He looked from her to me, smiled and explained that 'Jenny's a musicologist. Does not play an instrument herself but knows a lot about every single one of them. She's been following us around. Perhaps you noticed. Because she's received a grant from the Arts Council, the body which, I should remind you, pays a substantial part of your salary. She's been given this money to write a book, but I'll leave her to tell you all about it.'

Bertie then proceeded to give his own short summary that was sufficient to puncture my bloated vanity: she was not a groupie after all and had not been following me personally around the country. But before I was completely deflated, Bertie applied a patch to the hole he'd created in my fantasy: 'She's paying special attention to the wind section and within that to her own favourite instrument, the clarinet. She was just mentioning you when, lo and behold, you came up and joined us.'

The three of us chatted for a while until Bertrand finally excused himself and actually did go off to fulfil his diplomatic duties as orchestra manager, leaving us to continue our conversation. I regaled her with anecdotes from my repertoire of bizarre and hilarious events that I had encountered when on tour, which she genuinely seemed to find funny. When it was time to go we agreed that we should meet again in London, where we both lived.

Two months later we had lunch together at the Café Royal in Regent Street. I had in the past been infatuated by other women, but never before enthralled. Towards the end of the meal, both of us having consumed a considerable amount of wine, I could not resist asking her an intimate question. She did not blush and understood what I meant. 'Yes,' she said. I had put my marital cards on the table, telling her that I was married and had two grown-up sons. She smiled, put one hand on mine and one finger to her lips and invited me to go to her flat for coffee.

Approaching my fiftieth birthday, I was almost exactly twice her age; I was attracted to her youthful vitality and playfulness, the sensuousness of her moist, smooth, unlined skin and her tiny body. From the beginning I was overwhelmed by her sexual aggressiveness, gyrating on me until collapsing on my chest in her ecstasy, always ensuring that her needs were satisfied in our ravenous feasting on each other. Her attraction to me? I was content to drop anchor in the haven of the older man's fantasy; compared with her male peers I was urbane, romantic yet worldly, unassertively self-confident, and a considerate lover who pulsated to her lust.

I had had a few affairs in the past, but all of them, bar one, were best described for both of us as a pleasantly casual fling with a bit of rumpy-pumpy thrown in; the sex did not normally amount to much and it was not uncommon to return to the hotel after a good supper and fall asleep instead of having the anticipated uncommitted frolicky romp. A dentist's receptionist called Daphne was the sole exception; after a few months she began to treat our trysts as expressions of something more deep-seated and permanent; when that happened our relationship came to an abrupt end. Magda had known about a couple of the women and guessed both rightly and wrongly about others, but they were never a matter for discussion between us and I never enquired about any possible infidelities on her part.

Now, for the first time, I felt sorry for Magda. But

that, sadly, was all. By common consent much of our lives together had been spent in the shade, for the brightness of the sun never seemed to touch us. Our marriage had been alright, normal; we had, one might say, sailed the sea of marital life on an even keel. After more than a quarter of a century my relationship with Magda could best be described as commensal. The marriage had begun with no feelings or expressions of ecstasy and it was ending without any wailing. With Jenny nothing could have been more different; from the very beginning we basked and danced in the warmth of our own energy-generating aura.

Being so sexually explicit is for me difficult terrain, which I am nervous and reluctant to traverse. I am now having to overcome my inhibition in order to make one point clear: Jenny and I were mutually attracted to one another and the pleasure we derived from each other was reciprocal; however, all relationships contain imbalances so that one person is more dominant than the other in a particular aspect, which may, but usually does not, change over time. In our case, one of the fixed imbalances where Jenny dominated – in the sense of getting her way – was in the potent realm of sex.

I moved out from our comfortable home, leaving virtually everything behind; I was shedding my skin like a lizard escaping a predator to grow another while revelling in someone else's sunlight. I did not bother to look for somewhere to live by myself, as a station stop on my journey, but went straight to my destination, moving into Jenny's small flat. Money was short, the divorce expensive and irksome; I felt no acrimony or bitterness, though Magda did. Yet, her grief was not for my absence or for my withdrawal of love, because, sorry to say, there was no love left between us to be withheld or to be lost; she held me in contempt because of the stigma of the 'abandoned wife' that society had placed upon her.

Our sons were grown up and had left home. Julian, the elder of the two, had joined an architects' practice, which always seemed to have commissions, including several rewarding museum projects. His brother Ralph worked for a large firm of accountants and it was clear from his professional and private life that he had inherited his mother's managerial skills. Although sympathetic towards their mother's situation, they refused to take sides, except for the odd obliquely censorious comment that Ralph might make during one of our occasional lunches together. Their time for marital discord was yet to come. For my part, in Jenny I had someone to share my fretful moments and parings of sadness that I was the source of Magda's unhappiness. At the same time, of course, the melodrama of a fractured conjugal relationship and the drama of divorce added another line of stitches to our embroidered bed linen.

Jenny became pregnant during the first months of our living together. I wanted her to have the child, perhaps the first of two or three. But the idea of being a mother did not appeal to her – this was a subject that only ever came up incidentally; it was mentioned *en passant* rather than as a topic that merited the setting aside of time for serious discussion. In terms of importance, conversations about babies had the status of a stand-up snack rather than a sit-down meal.

At this stage Jenny would not tolerate any restriction on our dyadic freedom and greedy togetherness to eat out, entertain and travel untrammelled by offspring. Above all, she was jealously protective of her professional career, and so she had an abortion, which she arranged. It was on this occasion that I told her about Judith when I was at school. I suppose that the way in which I recounted the story sounded too flippant, for I was given more than a gentle rap over the knuckles; the event was never mentioned again nor were there any more 'accidents'. And we moved to another, larger flat.

After a few years, as the excitement and romance of our twosomeness reduced to a leisurely walking pace, she changed her mind. I recall the exact moment at which the turning point occurred. We had gone to friends for supper – her friends really, for they belonged to her generation. Our hostess, Charlotte, an interior designer, had invited us and another couple to see their first new-born baby. She spoke about her tiredness and discomforts and foresaw the difficulties of balancing the child's needs with her job. But as we drove home what we recalled and what stood out in our memories most vividly as we chatted about the evening were not our sighs and groans about how much she compressed into a typical day, but the sound of bells pealing the joy she felt when suckling her tiny, demanding creation.

Little more than a week after that evening, Jenny, now in her late thirties, raised the question of us starting a family. Now it was my turn to express reservations: the early urge on my part to become a father again had long since faded; it was an idea that had had its day. Besides, I was now a grandfather and so had enough babies and small children with whom to play and be photographed.

When my parents died, within a year of each other, I inherited a modest estate, including their eighteenth-century rectory in Shropshire, which we refurbished using part of my legacy. It was ideally located just a ten-minute drive from a railway station that had excellent rail connections to London. We moved in just before Jenny's fortieth birthday and, as usual, she took full responsibility for the interior furnishing. I bought her a pedigree Labrador Retriever as a birthday present and a comfortable car so that I could drive us both to the station. Although I had reached retirement age, I had managed to sign a contract with my orchestra for a further two years. Many of my friends thought that the music director had been tremendously generous and called me a lucky bastard. I agreed that the renewal was a stroke of good luck, though not undeserved.

Throughout our time together, Jenny's high standing within the profession, which stemmed from her wide-ranging knowledge of music, energy and consummate talent as an administrator, meant that she was much sought after, especially by commissioning males who, besides appreciating her ability to get things done, enjoyed the company of an extremely attractive and evidently sensual woman who possessed such unaffected, effortless charm.

We mainly went up to London together but, if she were going alone, since she had never learned to drive, I would take her to the station. Well, it's not entirely true that she'd never learned to drive, since we'd actually paid for her to have driving lessons. Unfortunately, she had failed her test not just once but twice – a fact she tauntingly blamed on me, saying that I had always found excuses for not giving her enough opportunity to practise. Now, to be fair, the charge had some substance to it and was one I had never challenged. I sincerely believed that there was something in her temperament – an apprehensiveness under certain circumstances – that could make her too hesitant and therefore, potentially, a driver dangerous to herself. And so, for her safety, despite the inconvenience it could sometimes cause me, I reckoned that it would be better for her to rely on me to get around by car.

Regrettably, the one thing she could increasingly no longer depend on me for was sex; although I remained sexually active, in one way or another, my desire for her lacked the old passion – and she most probably felt the same. The fire that we had enjoyed for so many years, though not extinguished, now only occasionally glowed, and, I am sad to say, very rarely flared.

Friends, quite a number with a musical background, used to come for weekends, and during the summer for longer stays. The ten years we spent in the rectory were richly lived and enjoyed, but time was ticking by and I was now well advanced into my third age. Although we continued to go for long, strenuous walks, life had quietened down; fewer of our older friends came to visit since they too had to adjust their routines to their physical capabilities – travelling seems to demand much more effort as we notch up the years – and to familial obligations that roll in on the swell of this stage in the life-cycle. Plainly, we were living in a property with far more rooms than we needed; on top of that, the costs of maintenance were rising, my savings were diminishing and the pension insufficient to cover all our expenses.

After batting the idea around for about a year we sold the house, a paragon of Georgian proportionality, and bought something much smaller: a newly built, detached house, one of a dozen or so, on an estate on the outskirts of a market town about eighty miles away. Ours was the very last one at the bottom of Prince's Lane, so called because of the area's association with a senior member of the royal family; years later, for reasons that will become very clear, the press dubbed it 'Prince of Darkness Lane'. The asphalted road ended outside our garage, which we could enter through the house. A public footpath ran down the side of the house and across a narrow strip of land into a coppice, beyond which the local council had set aside a patch of land for allotments that adjoined a couple of acres of wasteland.

Before purchasing, we received the assurance of a well-established firm of surveyors with good connections to the county council that no further development permits would be granted anywhere near our property. Their confidence was based on the fact that not only were the allotments protected but the wasteland was too badly polluted; it had once been the site of a chemical engineering factory which, after many years of depositing harmful waste on the adjacent land, had been forced to close down. Because of its toxicity, the local council had for a number of years resourcefully used it as the town's refuse tip until they were forced by new county ordinances to abandon the site.

Our new habitat was in stark contrast to our former, rectory home, but it suited both of us, though for different reasons: being able easily to walk into the town, Jenny quite literally found her feet in our new environment, quickly making friends and in no time joining a choral society and reading group; for my part I found the upkeep of the smaller space less time consuming.

The move brought home to us, separately, something we never mentioned: our age difference, which was coming to manifest itself in more and more ways. (Jenny had for some time jokingly reproached me for dropping off in the chair after lunch and again after supper.) It made no difference that I took exercise, had a healthy diet, hardly touched alcohol and had a good genetic inheritance; for, despite my lifestyle correctness, the old reaper now appeared more regularly in my dreams, though thankfully in disguise and not yet leading the allegorical *Totentanz* across the horizon with his ghastly smile.

After twenty-five years every spouse has heard the other's stock of tales so many times that when one of them begins to tell a story in company, the other stares abstractedly into the distance or faddishly picks at their food like a pecking hen. For the person walking in step with a coeval towards the grave, the tedium that is revived when the tale is recounted can sometimes – if you allow the hyperbole – make the grave seem just that little bit less unattractive than listening to the story yet again. For those in intergenerational liaisons, the monotony of the repetition may become unbearably exasperating with the result that the younger of the two comes to feel like a trapped child summoning the courage to leave the nest; having been fed and protected, the offspring knows that the time has come to fly. It is the 'parent' in the relationship who has to swallow hard and acknowledge the wisdom of the German poet's words that 'it is the duty of parents to give their children two things: roots and wings'.

I was vaguely aware of a duality of this sort, though I could never have expressed it with Goethe's elegant pithiness. I had certainly helped Jenny put down roots. But, to give her wings, well, while it might have been kind, saintly and altruistic to do so, frankly, from my point of view, it would have been an act of self-destructive madness; I was not her father but her husband and also, even if now rarely, her lover. My defensive device was simply to refuse to accept that she was able to look after herself. So, naturally, our tiffs, when they occurred, usually stemmed from her decrying my caring concern as really a cover for my need to control her; and the prime example that she liked to cite was my not doing more to help her pass her driving test.

When we moved to our new home Jenny had reached the age that I had been when we met. Then I was nudging middle age, experienced, a charged engine; now, that's what she was. I sought solace in the thought that I had played a good hand of three card brag and continued to do so to the best of my ability. However, naturally, my game was no longer what it had been and I had long ago used up all my trump cards. Just as I had at school and at college acknowledged that, basically, I would always be a mediocrity, now I reluctantly conceded that good old Charlie Brown had exhausted the jokers in the pack and simply had no more tricks to play.

As I already mentioned, not long after we had settled in our new home, Jenny had joined a choral society, to which she added membership of two other local clubs and a more distant operatic society; she was branching out and expressed an interest in becoming a *répétiteur* of all things. I knew I had no right to try to prevent her from taking the branch line from our track and never tried to fix the points. On the contrary, to show my love and attentiveness to her happiness, I invariably drove her to an event, then left and later returned to pick her up. Occasionally she'd be picked up by another group member and brought back by the same or a different person.

One may try to bury or banish unpleasant thoughts, but reality does not change as a consequence. I could only wait. Then, it happened. We had commissioned the installation of new windows and a small conservatory. The builder was a local man and the price was right. One day I caught them on the car bonnet in the garage *in delicto* – just like all those years ago when I was caught by my half-sister, but we had only been kissing.

The school I had attended for twelve years had achieved one of its primary goals for I had remained a Quaker in spirit and from time to time, when convenient (and on occasion when not so convenient), I used to go to meetings of the Society of Friends. Now that there was a Friends' House actually in the town, I became a more regular attendee. It was a place where I could refresh my trust in Reason as a good way to confront Adversity and surmount Problems, as I had done during my divorce from Magda. I replayed moments of that separation, remembering how at the time my feelings were more of uneasiness and regret for the situation that I had caused rather than compassion for the person affected: Magda.

After the revelation in the garage, Jenny and I sat down quietly, as couples can do under these circumstances, and rummaged around in our past, picking out and musing over the good times and skipping circumspectly over those that were not so good. The breakdown of our marriage – and that's what we agreed had happened – turned on one basic fact: he was twenty years younger than me and thus a member of her generation and full of life. To put it crudely, from my point of view, admittedly somewhat jaundiced, he was full of fucking life, if you understand what I mean (and generously pardon the pun and my use of the word) even if devoid of much else. Because I could never bring myself to mention his name, I referred to him as 'Lovely Job', as that is how he referred to his work – 'Now that's what I call a lovely job' – and that is precisely how I imagined she referred to what he did to her.

The whole affair, from my discovering her fully clothed and straddled by LJ over the car bonnet to her deciding to leave me, lasted about six weeks. We agreed that the house should be sold and the income from the sale divided equally; the normally vexatious issue of the distribution of its contents went smoothly, with scarcely a bicker and no demonstration of animosity. The only slightly upsetting aspect of our amicably arranged settlement was that she did not want to take the dog – not the Labrador I had given to her as a gift, for he was long gone, but an ungainly mongrel bitch that we had acquired just a few months earlier from the local dogs' home. Thus, overall, apart from a few minor misunderstandings, the conduct of the formal dissolution of our relationship was quaintly civilised and after the major decisions had been taken, we could smile at each other and give each other the occasional, reserved peck or hug. We had entered, as anyone who has gone through a divorce knows, uncharted waters that can be murky, muddy, calm or turbulent and at times cruel.

As the day Jenny was due to move out approached,

we agreed that the two of us should spend the evening together at home in Prince's Lane, in order to exhale a final goodbye. I was struck by the fact that Jenny, unlike me, who had walked out of my shared home with Magda and straight into the flat of my new lover, had decided to spend a metaphorical forty days alone. The quarantine would, she had said, give her time and space to reflect on our life as a couple before crossing the threshold into a new existence with Lovely Job.

Amongst our friends and neighbours it was common knowledge that, consistent with the dignified manner in which we had handled the parting of our ways, I would be dropping Jenny off at the station in a nearby village to catch the early morning express to London, where she had the key to the flat of one of her oldest friends who had gone abroad to work for an indeterminate period and did not want to rent the flat out through an agency. Jenny was to make a contribution to the flat's upkeep during her projected forty-day stay and, thereafter, whenever she might wish to have a break, until the owner's return when her contract expired.

Unfortunately, our quiet fireside evening never materialised, for by the time she came through the door after visiting the friend who had been her principal confidant, she was looking the worse for wear. Although she was smiling, her lips twitched and her normally twinkling eyes looked like protruding, glazed marbles. She slumped into a chair, dropping her handbag beside her, kicked off her shoes and said, 'Why do you always look so bloody miserable, James? You're like a wet rag.

Sorry, flannel. You should go out and enjoy yourself.'

James? She had never once called me that before. My bewilderment quickly escalated into apprehension.

'The problem for me, and for you too, is that you're not the man I married,' she continued.

'I haven't changed. I am the same person I've always been,' I replied slowly, disinclined to antagonise her during the final hours of our cohabitation.

'Well, perhaps that's the problem,' she said, her eyes rolling. 'And do you know why it's a problem? It's because you're a wimp.'

My puzzlement and dread were racing; I could not understand where the venom was coming from. Was the person saying such hateful things about me to my face the real Jenny, whose true self had for so many years been buried, or simply concealed from me? Or, was this the mask she wanted to wear or thought that, in the circumstances, she ought to wear? It had been a long time since the idea of 'true self' had arisen as a question to torment me. Like so many existential questions that bump into us as we walk along, or jump down and squash us when we are sitting quietly or rear up nightmarishly just as we switch off the light to climb into bed, they tend to besiege us when we are growing up (say, up until we are roughly fifty years old) not when we are growing old, after the age of sixty.

My mind scuttled around foraging amongst the optional answers to the questions that had been raised in the last few minutes. It came to rest on the thought that, in her view, since she was being a hurtful bastard she ought to behave like one and act out the role that had been scripted for her. More or less at the same time, my body tautened and my shoulders hunched up as they had when I responded as a conscript to the bellow of a sergeant-major. My consciousness, which trod one step behind my body's physical reaction, when it caught up, pounced on the name she'd called me.

Our very last night together and she calls me James. Why? I had always been Jimmy to her since we'd met; and for a long time before that I had been known as 'Charlie Brown'. My name was my identity – informal, easy-going and always ready for fun. By saying 'James' she was not just assaulting my identity, but plainly seeking to change the very person I felt myself to be. Yes, she had negated me, nullified me; I was not a James but a Jimmy. And, now, she is accusing me of being a wimp – a term so much more hurtful than 'you fucker', because while the former emasculates, the latter, perversely, in this usage, implies the opposite. Saying that a man is a wimp falls into the same category of emasculatory language as calling a man 'nice', a term that reduces a man to the status of a bonbon, a *dolce* – a 'sweetie'. In fact, in a sudden flashback to a moment not so long ago, before 'the revelation', I recalled how, during a genial evening on the sofa together she'd called me 'nice'; now I was a wimp. She had written me off as a male! I felt more than offended; she had scarred and defaced me.

As my ego absorbed this disfigured portrait of myself, I folded my arms, leant forward and looked into her rolling eyes and said, 'Oh, come on, Jenny, you're pissed, why don't you go to bed? We've got an early start tomorrow.'

'Alright, yes, I am pissed, and you're as bloody sober as ever.' She slumped back and then pulled herself forward and blurted out, 'At least I don't have to sleep in the same bed.' This was followed by a burst of bilious bitterness. I squinted as she pushed herself up on the padded arms of her favourite wing chair. She made it up the stairs and I collapsed back into the well-worn brocaded chesterfield, picking up the newspaper from the side-table, as if words had the power to distract me from the ambient decay.

Having swallowed whole columns in a glance without digesting the meaning of a single sentence, I let the broadsheets slip out of my hands onto my outstretched legs. I remember feeling my exhausting unhappiness flow out of me and then after a while getting up and walking into the tidy, spotlessly clean kitchen where I poured myself a glass of water.

Standing at the sink, shifting from foot to foot, I stared out into the darkness picking out in the pale light of a crescented moon the shadows of the trees at the bottom of the garden. Eventually I ceased sighing and, shaking my head, walked up the stairs leadenly like a somnambulist and into Jenny's bedroom, where she had managed to undress and crawl under the covers. She was dead to the world, metaphorically speaking. I picked up a very large cushion and pressed it down on her face with my full body weight; soon she was dead, literally. Not wanting to see her eyes I pulled the sheet over the head as I pulled the cushion away.

Throughout the break-up, through our pleading with one another – mine to her to stay and hers to me to release her – through the occasional burst of tears, neither of us had been physically violent or verbally abusive to the other. Even during my bleakest moments the idea of hurting Jenny had never insinuated itself onto any of my multiple lists of possible courses of action. My action therefore was an aberration, so that even today after all these years, I can honestly declare that I never had any intention of occasioning her death. But, at the same time, to be absolutely candid, I had no intention whatsoever of confessing to anyone what I had done and placing myself at the mercy of the law. Suddenly my body began to shiver and my hands tremble – out of fear not remorse; there was no time to allow feelings of guilt, grief, regret and so on to elbow their way in and hamper me from concentrating all my attention on surviving.

I wrapped Jenny's body in a blanket and carried it out through the back door, down the garden and on to the path leading to the allotment, where, on buying the house, I had quickly secured a plot with a tiny shed, inside which was a small wheelbarrow and spade. As I pushed my Snow White to her tumulus, I swayed to my whistling of the dwarfs' hi-ho hi-ho song. Today, thinking back to that particular moment in the chain of events, I can honestly say I am horrified at my macabre behaviour, ghoulish choice of tune and the fact that I chuckled as I barrowed her body to what was, after all, the rubbish dump.

Afterwards I returned home, and just before six o'clock, the world still deeply wrapped in autumnal darkness, I took the car out of the garage and drove to the station. I parked in a narrow, overgrown lane leading to a derelict barn, put on Jenny's raincoat, hat and shoes, and walked the remaining distance to the station, strolling in front of the window of the waiting room where a solitary man would subliminally register a woman passing by. I went behind the railway building and made my way back to the car and drove home.

A month later, her body decomposing under the wasteful weight of others' refuse, I thought it would be a good idea to phone Lovely Job.

'Harvey,' I said, 'have you heard anything from Jenny yet? I know she wanted to spend time by herself' – I paused, sipped my tea and crunched a shortbread biscuit, almost certain that as soon as we put our receivers down, he would scream out 'wanker' at the picture he would have of me in my armchair, and continued – 'but she did say she'd be in touch and I haven't heard a word.' I pronounced my words like an actor performing in *An Ideal Husband*, articulating every syllable slowly and deliberately so that Wilde would receive the applause that his lines deserve.

'No, I haven't,' he replied brusquely, almost implying that I was in some way responsible for his not having received any communication from her. 'She asked me to let her alone for a while and that's what I am doing.'

'I suppose you're right. But, if she does contact you, please ask her to give me a ring, just so that I know everything is alright. I still care about her. Goodbye then.' I put down the receiver and bit my tongue; I had said 'if' not 'when' she contacted him. I could feel my heart palpitating at what was a gross mistake on my part, but the beat reduced to normal by the time I had finished my tea, placated by my conviction that Harvey would never remember whether I had said 'if' or 'when'.

Another couple of weeks passed and, not having heard from Lovely Job, I called him again, expressing my anxiety at such a long silence. We both knew the reason for his brooding reluctance to ring the police and it was not because he lacked the wit to contact them and thus start the process of having Jenny elevated to missing person status. No, it was another case of social class, for although we were estranged, Jenny and I remained, as we always had been, a law-abiding, professional, middle-class couple. On the other hand, Harvey Harvester – Lovely Job's real name – came from a large extended family, one or two of whose members were quite well known to the police; so, not surprisingly, LJ, as an adulterer, did not want to be the person to initiate contact with the law. That is why the task fell to me.

My life during the weeks between Jenny's death (I never called it murder) and the police knock on the door continued as normal. My relationship with the neighbours and their behaviour towards me stayed the same; and with those who knew Jenny more intimately the conversation often turned on wondering what she might be doing in London. The sun rose and set, I shopped, worked on my allotment, and at night slept peacefully. I bleached and rinsed out the whole affair with what I considered infallible logic: I could not be held responsible for her death, nor, therefore, should I be punished for it.

The police duly went to the London flat and, since there was no evidence of her ever having been there, both LJ and I became prime suspects and implicated in her disappearance. During my interviews with the police, I presented myself as a paragon of liberal middle England and a modest septuagenarian Quaker to boot. The inquest opened and closed; Jenny was declared a 'missing person' and I was left alone by the outside world, which tended to look at LJ with suspicion and upon me with pity.

When you reach a certain age, living alone can be lonely. Yet, I never missed Jenny because by the time of our separation, we were journeying along the same road at different speeds; the asymmetry in our ages had come to matter. However, I had no yearning to have a live-in companion closer to me in years; just too much baggage: apart from family there would be the things she liked to eat, when she was habituated to do the washing up, how thoroughly she rinsed the dishes, for how long she brushed her teeth and how badly she splashed the mirror, and at what time she went to bed. The same prosaic decisions have to be made whether living alone or with another person – only in the case of the former, the choices are less open to disputation. All this sounds trivial, but it is the stuff of daily existence.

I dreamt a lot, but only ever remembered one of my

dreams. I was in full evening dress, presumably after a performance, standing on the harbourside of a small port on a Mediterranean island. It was summer and late at night. But instead of small fishing boats bobbing in still, oily water, the backdrop to the scene was a naval barracks and victualling yard constructed from massive limestone blocks. It seemed as if the place was under occupation and a curfew had been imposed, for the quay was deserted. I walked around the harbour towards a jetty in the middle of which there was a wrought-iron gate, with no wall, barbed wire or any other form of obstruction on either side; it looked like a stage prop around which anyone could walk.

A young-looking woman and athletically built man of about the same age approached the gate where they were challenged by a guard who told them that they were not allowed to go any further. The woman kept talking and tried to ease past him; as the guard turned to his side to pull her back, the male companion produced a knife and stabbed him in the back. Seeing this I rushed out of the shadows and drew out my own weapon – a tin whistle – and blew it. But there was no sound. I blew again and this time I saw notes floating out of the instrument in the form of feathers, which began to dance. The couple turned around and trance-like began to skip after the feathers that were flowing in a line towards the end of the jetty. The notes continued over the water and the man and woman plunged down into it.

For three years I lived a sedate, contented, though basically humdrum, bachelor life, now and again seeing children, grandchildren and the odd old relative or friend, and keeping abreast with international, national and local news. I had always had a strong civic conscience and read about and supported local causes, occasionally through small donations; at the same time, I seldom attended civic events, such as public meetings or performances by our amateur thespians. Jenny, as you may have gathered, was the direct opposite: outward going and engaging, an active member of the community. After she had exited from my life, passed on, as it were, I slowly began to replace the small vacuum that she had left in the community by a series of small initiatives.

My only successful idea was the placing of an advertisement in the window of the newsagent located in the main square and in the town's *Mercury and Courier*, offering my services as a tutor for young musicians. Since I regarded what I wanted to do as strictly *pro bono publico*, I did not want to charge for my time. But such is the spirit of the age in which we live, a Friend cautioned me that anyone – especially an old man – doing something for nothing that also involved young people would be viewed with considerable suspicion. Alerted to this horrible possibility, I set my fee at a level somewhere below what I ascertained was the market level and specified that I was only qualified to assist students who were interested in playing woodwind instruments.

The response was very gratifying; I had students of all ages, despite the fact that I had initially stipulated that applicants should be 'young'. The teaching was so rewarding and revitalising that it extended my lease on life. After a couple of months the number of pupils stabilised at a baker's dozen, drawn from the town and neighbouring villages. One of them was a sixteen-year-old girl, Helen. She was serious about her music and played in the school orchestra. Although the school music teacher gave her extra tuition, because she was a clarinettist, he had encouraged her to take extra lessons from someone who played the instrument.

I had started giving classes at the beginning of the school year and just before the Christmas break during my mid-week lesson with Helen I noticed that she was not concentrating on her playing.

'Is everything alright, Helen?' I asked.

'Yes, thank you,' she replied, 'but would you mind if I finished early this evening, I just don't feel well?'

'No, of course not. There's no sense in putting yourself through the paces if you're not up to it. I can see you next week and you can have a longer lesson.' She smiled, packed her clarinet and left. The following week, a day before she was due to come, she phoned to say that she was still not feeling well and asked if she could cancel the forthcoming lesson. Our brief conversation about her school work, the preparations for the Christmas concert in which she was going to perform a solo and the coming vacation were interspersed with her apologies for her behaviour. We agreed to meet again in the New Year. She sent me a seasonal greetings card thanking me for all the help that I had given her and for being so understanding.

That year the weeks around Christmas were particularly hectic and I only turned to thinking about my returning students a week before they were due to start. I looked at my list and thought about the strengths and weaknesses of each of them. Helen would be my fourth student of the new term. When she arrived I immediately sensed that she had changed in some way. When she took off her coat and sat down the nature of the change became clear.

'How are you, Helen? How was Christmas? Did you enjoy the holiday?' I asked with a concerned voice.

'Oh, everything was fine. Just the usual,' she said in a matter-of-fact way with a bare smile and took out her music.

After a quarter of an hour of practising, she sat down. 'I wonder if I could have a glass of water, please, Mr Brown,' she said.

'Yes, coming right up,' I said as breezily as I could. She drained the glass, breathed out heavily, smiled again, stood up and resumed playing.

As we approached the end of the session, I could see her flagging. 'Would you like to stop now? You do look quite exhausted. A cup of tea before you leave?'

'Yes, I am and yes to that too, thank you,' Helen replied and as her mouth opened to smile more fully her eyes watered.

For the first time in almost fifty years I thought of Judith.

'You're pregnant, aren't you?' I asked bending down towards her.

'Yes. You can tell, can you?' She asked like a child who has dirtied her new dress.

'Are you going to keep it?' I enquired, burrowing where perhaps I shouldn't.

'I don't know,' she answered calmly raising her eyebrows.

As I closed the door behind her, a tear welled up and I began to sob, gently at first and then uncontrollably.

Like most people, I did not take that much interest in discussions surrounding proposals to change laws that did not directly affect me, knowing full well that big issues can be bandied about by politicians, civil servants and various so-called stakeholders for years before legal teams finally draft legislation. Eventually the Bill becomes an Act of Parliament and people are compelled to comply with it or avail themselves of its provisions.

One such case, which seemed to stroll through committees in the Palace of Westminster and Whitehall departments for ever, was legislation to change the rules regulating where new housing could be built. As far as I was concerned, reforms to the planning norms and the shift towards brown-field development sat alongside other issues that were peripheral to my daily existence, drifting around in the stratosphere and very distant from me – until one morning when I read in the local press that the county council, short of cash, had agreed to sell its abandoned refuse tip to a developer.

Then, as is often the case, all went silent and little more was heard of the project to build on the toxic site. Naturally, there were buckets of gossip, whose sources were usually traceable to the various interested parties and their legal representatives arguing for and against the principle of the project and then debating its details.

The actual ground-moving moment – literally, if you will pardon the rather bad joke – came during a heatwave in August. I shall never forget the serenity and tranquillity of that early morning as I returned from the newsagent with my monthly copy of *The Contemporary Museum Curator* and a pint of milk, the grass necklaced with dew and bushes linked by filigreed cobwebs and the sun pale in the powder blue sky; it was under these paradisiacal conditions that I saw a mechanical digger inscribed with my initials, JCB, trundle down the road towards the tip. From my first sighting of my eponymous nemesis I was able to plot the course leading to my demise that would be as inevitable as had been Jenny's.

My trial lasted fifteen weeks; its cultured conduct was only marred by the court cartoonist's crayon drawing of me standing in the dock, which I still have amongst my papers, because he managed to make me resemble an artist's sketched portrait of Eichmann at his trial in Jerusalem.

As you might have expected, I presented the local journalists with a once-in-a-lifetime *cause célèbre*, which engrossed their inquisitional attention long after the jury had reached its verdict. Not so for the hacks from the national press, whose interest waned quite quickly. Nevertheless, coverage of an alleged murder of a woman by her much older husband had attracted those journalists from Europe and further afield, who considered the case would appeal to the interests of certain segments of their readership – many of whom had already judged me to be a heinous misogynist or were themselves maggoty voyeurs.

For most of the time I averted my eyes from the courtroom spectators, but occasionally I let them drift aimlessly over the benches. Whenever I caught the gaze of one of Jenny's relatives and friends or the sad, quizzical look of other people I recognised, I turned away in smouldering embarrassment because of my deceit and betrayal of trust. I saw Magda sitting in the back row of the court on day one; when our eyes met, she just shook her head slowly from side to side and I thought that I could read on her moving lips the words 'You silly fool'.

Julian, who was by then himself divorced, also popped in on the opening day and attended the summing-up session, on both occasions communicating with me with his mobile face. The staid Ralph, who was anchored to a moping wife, took pains to write me a pious, but still considerate and caring, letter. Just as with my break-up with their mother, I cannot complain about their conduct.

Then, on the third day, I noticed sitting in the front row a woman dressed in a tailored grey costume with a tightly fitting jacket, decorated with green piping and two green stripes on the lapels, opened over a white, daintily embroidered blouse that enclosed a huge bosom. As the prosecution droned on, my concentration, already dwindling from *ennui*, switched from the proceedings to the woman in grey who, catching my eye, smiled and nodded. I looked back again and we stared into each other's blue sensories; it was Eva, whom I hadn't seen, so we later calculated, for twenty-six years.

What life I have left was saved by the psychobabble of the psychiatrist who had been commissioned by my defence barrister to explain in the most sympathetic way possible why I had murdered my wife. He produced, like a seaside pier magician, a syndrome from which he said I was palpably suffering; in fact, he regarded me as a classic case of the illness. At the word 'illness' I pricked up my ears; I did not feel ill and certainly was not ill when I smothered Jenny. But no, he described with some pathos just how unfortunate was the person who stood in front of the court and jury; he invoked instances of the syndrome, which had only recently been identified and which had been used to explain other famous and equally puzzling cases of uxoricide in the ancient past and more recently. The particular speech which saved me, when pared down to its essence, stated that it was

Jenny's taunting and humiliating remark, calling me a wimp, possibly made off the cuff when drunk, that had been our damnation.

He was a mild-mannered man in his early forties, clearly losing his hair out of the worries he bore on his shoulders for the unlucky and the doomed. He was persuasive but not suave, convincing but not overbearing; he was the modern, bland Anglican vicar addressing his flock and all but used the words 'he who would cast the first stone' and 'there but for the grace of God go I'. It was the professional opinion of the man in the serge suit not in the barrister's silk that persuaded the jury and judge to set my retribution at three years of deprived liberty in an open prison.

Eva visited me regularly during the twelve months that I served before being released. We conversed in German and I learned much more about my half-sister and her family. Birgit, who was still alive, regretted that she was too old and frail to travel to see me; instead we communicated by letter. In one she jokingly reminded me of how, when we had first met, I had proudly announced that, in contrast to her, I had been brought up in the violence-eschewing Quaker tradition.

Shortly after my discharge I went to visit them in Baiersdorf, where I was introduced to other people as Jakob Braunsteig. My first visit to my father's homeland had been as an inquisitive, rather gauche, young man who felt and behaved like an outsider. The subsequent occasional family exchanges had been little more than holidays with long-standing friends. Now, well past the three score and ten post, I had returned not just to my father's roots but to my own, to a place where it seemed natural to be; I felt welcomed as an insider, one who has been outside for a long time.

Nevertheless, I decided that I couldn't, after so many years, remain in the nest from which my father had flown and thus I returned to England. But I did so as Jakob Braunsteig, as I told you at the beginning. This gave me the persona of someone deeply attached to people and places other than the village and country in which I was born and again live. Interestingly, when in prison I read about a neurological test that was used to determine a person's primary language. It's quite simple: you ask the person being tested to close their eyes and count to ten. Then when they open their eyes again you ask them in which language they counted. I took the test and the result was that I counted in German.

2

Foreign Correspondence

'Joyless' was the word that best described Morgan's train journey that had begun in Wien Westbahnhof and ended at Liverpool Street station. For most of those twelve hours he had been preoccupied with what had gone wrong during the week they had spent together. Since they had not seen one another for months, it was not surprising that they should feel a little awkward, uneasy and even tense in each other's company. Yet, he should have known from the reunion kisses on the platform – the first too hurried and the second artificially prolonged – that something more serious had happened in Astrid's life. Too much of their ten days together in the Tyrol had been taken up by more than the usual petty squabbling and fault finding, and no doubt she had felt, as he had, that their reconciliations lacked sincerity and the sex, when it happened, was as brief as it was contrived. Thinking back, perhaps he should have read more into her outright and, frankly, discourteous refusal to accept an invitation from a couple she had known for years to accompany them to an open-air concert; she had even admitted when pressed that the friends had been looking forward to seeing him again.

The day after his arrival back in England, Astrid had rung him at his office, much as he had anticipated and hoped. What he had not foreseen, following their exchange of self-righteous recriminations, was that she would tell him in her forthright way that they should stop seeing one another. She had met his spiritless protests with characteristic firmness. He knew her well enough to know that she would not relent once she had made her decision.

Because Astrid had been so icy and peremptory, the shock was glacial in its effect, forcing him first to freeze his emotions and then repress what was for him simultaneously a loss and rejection. If the sharp pain of the present had to be anaesthetised and put into cold storage, rather than rally his memory of the good times that they had spent together, he chose to allow even them to be swept away by a strong undercurrent of induced bafflement, pulled under and drowned.

As her directness had not been her most endearing feature – though it was one that he admired, particularly because he was the opposite – Morgan was brought face to face with what had been the foundation and later the keystone to their relationship: their sexual lust for one another. They hadn't laughed much together; it had been an effort to make a joke and generally be gay in each other's company. He knew that while she understood, smiled and appreciated his puns, she disliked the cynical and sarcastic edge to his view of the world. Apart from the outdoor life there were few other hobbies and interests that they shared. Therefore, when that keystone of carnal desire began to lose its ability to hold the two parts of the human bridge together, its rather bathetic end was easily predictable.

In the absence of a confessor, Astrid's decree gave him absolution and neither had to ask the other for forgiveness. He would do as Astrid had suggested: they should (an Astrid imperative) bundle up and tidy away their secret letters, put the affair behind them and continue their individual journeys. Putting her libido to one side, Astrid's behaviour and advice on this occasion seemed to him to epitomise her practical, matter-of-fact, coolly stoical approach to life.

Now, ten days later, he was making a much shorter train ride; this time from Fenchurch Street to Tilbury, accompanied by Charlie, one of his oldest friends. At the dock, the two of them made their way to a two-storey, *art deco*, 1930s red-brick building with classically modernist metal window frames. Inside, they sat at a small, square table with a yellow Formica top beneath an unattractive, greasy and smoke-stained chandelier. From this seedy rest for the seasoned traveller they could see the white funnel of the ship that Morgan was to sail in.

As embarkation time approached, Charlie broached the issue that, even as very good friends, they had avoided talking about.

'How does Janet feel about your being gone for such a long time?' he asked.

'I don't know,' was Morgan's immediate response. How could he know what his wife thought? It had all happened so quickly; during the spring they had taken themselves off for a weekend and, while browsing the Sunday newspapers after breakfast, he had seen and shown to her an advertisement for a one-year post to work abroad. Since his dissatisfaction with his work and career – epitomised in his stock phrase 'I'm stagnating' – was having an enervating effect on both their lives, they had nothing to lose if he submitted an application. Further discussion was deemed unnecessary until they knew whether or not he had been selected. Of course, when the letter arrived notifying him that his application had been successful it seemed obvious that he couldn't decline the offer.

After expressing her reservations about accepting the offer because of the long period they would be separated, Janet eventually deferred to his arguments for going ahead, while remaining silently unconvinced by his claim that this venture would benefit both of them, not just him. 'We'll show everyone how we've been able to escape the rut and not stay stuck where we are until we're eventually pensioned off,' he had declared euphorically.

'Everyone?' she had tried to challenge.

'Yes, everyone. Don't look so incredulous. Of course, there'll be the odd sod, like that Jeremiah, what's her name?'

'Leigh,' Janet had said with a groan. And that, basically, summed up their discussion of the issue.

Thereafter, their discussions of his decision to take the appointment had been confined to practicalities.

'When does she return from Italy?' Charlie hesitatingly probed, knowing that Janet and Morgan had spent a long summer holiday with friends in a rented villa in the Dolomites. Since she could work from there, he had travelled back alone to prepare for this trip, stopping off in Vienna on the way.

'If you like, I'll drop in on her when she gets back, just to make sure everything's alright and she's not too lonely.'

'Oh, I'm sure that she won't be lonely,' Morgan said almost with a sigh. 'You know as well as anyone that she enjoys her job immensely and lives a very busy professional life.' He paused for a moment, and added, 'Thanks, Charlie. That's really very kind and considerate of you. I'm sure she'd love to see you, or receive the odd call.'

'Can I just confirm,' Charlie said, 'you're back at the beginning of July? Is that correct?'

'Yep. Contract ends on 30 June. Must be back for the old anniversary.'

'Quite right too. I was thinking that yours more or less coincides with ours. The four of us could go out just as we did two years ago. In fact, we could turn the anniversary into a homecoming celebration.' Charlie reached over and slapped Morgan's arm.

'What a good idea,' Morgan answered with a lifeless smile but at the same time raising his glass to his friend.

As the two friends drained their glasses, Morgan

raised his eyes to look intently at Charlie's prematurely wrinkle-lidded eyes and said, 'You know, Charlie, believe it or not, I'm quite optimistic about the future really. As Sartre once wrote: "The world of the 'is' must always be criticised and challenged to reveal the possibilities within it". It's true. Think about it. It's such a good maxim that I've stuck it up as my motto on the pin-board next to our bed.'

There was a tea-sip of silence then Morgan continued with affected seriousness: 'You know what, my old friend, I've developed a certain rapport with the ceiling in our bedroom. It sees everything. Sometimes I crawl into bed, Janet's on her side facing away from me – into the wall with this pin-board – and I kiss her neck and caress her gently because she's told me it's something she likes me to do. After a while I roll over onto my back and stare at the off-white, woodchip-papered ceiling, which I can see in the light from the street lamp that filters through our threadbare, unlined curtains. Nothing very profound ever crosses my mind. I just ask myself, "Is this all that life's about?" A bit banal, don't you think?'

'No. It's not a banal question at all. That is what life's all about. Its ordinariness.' Charlie knew his lines by heart; this wasn't the first time that they'd trampled over this territory and he could have scripted his friend's next line.

'Don't give me that existentialist crap,' Morgan huffed out from puffed cheeks and pouted lips. 'Life is absurd. There's no doubt in my mind about that, but being doesn't have to be nothingness. We don't have

to live on a permanent plateau of stolid indifference.'
Morgan had a stern look on his face as he abruptly
finished speaking.

'Oh you are an old fart! You exaggerate everything.
Have you forgotten your Chesterton?' Charlie asked.

'Yes. But what in particular?'

'His neat aphorism: "the ecstasy of being ordinary".'

'Oh, bugger Chesterton. And, fart, yes. Old fart, no.
That will come with time.'

''Tis time to part,' Charlie rhymed. They both
laughed, stood up, walked out into the hazy September,
breathed in the fresh sea air, shook hands and embraced.

'You're a good man, Charlie,' Morgan said, then,
registering a moistening of his friend's eye, added,
'You're lucky to be so warm and affectionate. Or, should
I say, "I'm lucky that you are". And, not just me, but lots
of people.'

'Hang on, Morgan. Where's all this coming from?'

Morgan raised his eyebrows, waggled his shoulders
and went to board his ship. He found his cabin, deposited
his trunk and returned to the deck to wave to his friend;
since Janet couldn't be there to see him off, Charlie had
been determined that someone would.

Not a single cloud came into the sky throughout the
breezeless three-day voyage. Morgan spent most of that
time lazily and leisurely sitting in a deck chair; each
evening, with supper over, he retired to the same place

in the stern, watching darkness glide gracefully into blackness. After a while, and always at the same time, the ship reduced speed, muffling the sound of the turbines and reducing the vessel's vibration to a gentle throb that lulled the passengers to sleep.

Sitting alone, immersed in the stillness, he was fleetingly joined by friends, acquaintances and by the odd stranger with whom he had joked at a reception or whose hand he had shaken at an official event. Alternatively, a whole host of mystics, warrior-princes, popes, prophets and poets and sinning geniuses encountered in books and journals slipped out and danced, moaned and muttered in front of him. As they duelled and duetted, fêted and murdered, they appealed to him to understand why they had sacrificed their lives and those of others for their visions and beliefs. That they should want him to listen to their side of the story satisfied his propensity for uncomfortable facts to be explained and tidied up.

After disembarking, having his passport stamped by a pompous official and completing customs formalities, Morgan struggled with his luggage to the taxi rank, where his knowledge of the language, though flawed, helped him in the free-for-all to secure a cab to take him from the port to the railway station. Having found his train and reserved sleeping compartment, he placed his luggage under the bunk and made his way to the restaurant carriage and sat down at one of the few remaining tables for two. He gazed out into the darkness and, seeing nothing at all, moved his head until he found himself looking into his own eyes. Embarrassed, he turned to examine the faces of other passengers.

His eye settled on a middle-aged man with a large wart on his nose; it was the sort of minor disfigurement that made Morgan flinch, because he knew that were the two of them to have a conversation, his eye would uncontrollably dart to the wart where his stare would be trapped. Just at the moment when he grasped the Gogolian association between noses and warts, a waiter appeared and, without being asked, opened a bottle of mineral water. As Morgan picked it up to sip, an attractive woman about his age came into the carriage, approached a table, asked a question and retreated, the remaining chair obviously taken. She turned and came across to him.

'Excuse me, is this place free?' she asked. Each word was clearly pronounced and projected.

'Yes, it is,' he said welcomingly. A number of witty responses scampered through his head, but it was too late, the moment for a Samuel Johnson *bon mot* or Bogartian flirtatious quip had passed. She sat down. Eventually they ordered and were served. He made an unimaginative observation about the food and service; she responded with an anecdote about travelling and eating with strangers; he dug up an old joke which she parried. By the end of the meal they were talking and laughing like old friends. She told him that she didn't expect to get much sleep since she had to change trains in the middle of the night; while he was continuing to travel southward, her ultimate destination was further to the east.

She was familiar with the town where he would be staying, because a number of years ago she had spent the summer in a house situated in one of the oldest districts of this provincial centre. With its detached log and timber-framed houses surrounded by unruly gardens and cherry and apple orchards, it wasn't unusual for visitors to the neighbourhood to imagine that they were in an overgrown village rather than a town. She mentioned and recommended several walks in the vicinity, a few well known, others less so.

'I expect to be passing through your area in a few months' time. If you're free,' she said when she stood up to leave, 'we could take a trip to a villa where in the aftermath of a particular liaison a famous composer, who was also a notorious womaniser, had written his most famous cello concerto commonly referred to as the *River in Flood*. He actually died there during the typhoid epidemic at the beginning of the century. It's a museum now and since it's a couple of hours' drive from the centre of town, it's never too crowded.' On that note, they both stood up, shook hands and she left.

He was so busy during the first couple of weeks after his arrival in the town that he had no time to think about what he had left behind, or whether he was happy or sad, let alone about the co-passenger on the train. Then, one morning, coming slowly into consciousness, he found himself smiling; not about anything in particular. It was just a feeling of contentedness, which he didn't want to lose; he kept his eyes closed, turned over, pulled his legs up into a foetal position, and tugged the bed cover over his head.

He reminisced timelessly, roaming randomly over the past days, to the boat, to an event ten years earlier, then to one nearer in time. During the previous day not a cloud had slipped into or drifted across the blue sky; today was going to be the same he declared as he closed the door on his memories, jumped out of bed and pulled the curtains back to let the bright light swim in.

The reinvigorating effect of the blue canopy could be felt everywhere, so that when Morgan arrived at the small restaurant, where he usually went for lunch, he found that the vases on each of the five tables were full of freshly cut flowers. He sat down, put his newspaper on the windowsill and opened a letter he'd received that morning. It brought bad news: his mother's sister, his favourite aunt, had died; although he rarely saw her since moving to London, she always sent them cards on their birthdays. The letter, written by her daughter, explained that she had been in the room when her mother had collapsed from a massive heart attack, adding in her matter-of-fact and ironic way that at first she'd thought that her mother was choking on her false teeth. He searched himself for feelings, trying to find a word to match them, something like remorse, pity, sadness; but nothing seemed to fit.

Morgan folded the letter, replaced it in the envelope and hesitantly and self-consciously slid it into his pocket. He stood up leadenly and went to look at a photograph of a faded and badly framed still-life on the wall opposite. Suddenly struck by the contrast between the brilliance of the day outside and, despite the fresh flowers, the dullness of the atmosphere inside, he decided, as a gesture to his aunt's exuberance (and to compensate for his lack of demonstrable compassion), to celebrate her life rather than lament her death. He caught the waitress's eye and ordered a glass of wine instead of his usual espresso, sat back and browsed through a magazine. After a short time, he signalled to the waitress again; she came; he paid and left.

The news of his aunt's death was being wrapped in the deep, rich colours of a pleasantly warm autumn day; her burial would coincide with harvest festival. 'Yes,' he muttered aloud, as he reached the nearby smoothly flowing river, under whose banks the heaps of pebbles and ridges of sand were reminders of less tranquil seasons, 'even if you live to be a hundred, life is short, very, very short.'

The warmth and daytime haze of an early autumn, anti-cyclonic, waning sun is deceptive; shining through a tinted, but not yet turned, foliage, it tempts people to forget the month when choosing in the morning what clothes to wear. It was his favourite season: 'Seasons of mists and mellow fruitfulness/Close bosom-friend of the maturing sun.' Ah! Keats. Poor consumptive Keats. Morgan liked the word 'consumptive', deriving from the verb 'to consume', a word he associated with passion, as in 'a consuming passion'.

The thought prompted him to wonder why, over the course of their lives, apart from notable (more often, notorious) exceptions, human beings have so few consuming passions. He paused and pulled the emergency cord, bringing the train of thought to a halt, just as he turned into the town's old, though no longer main, square, which was on his way home. It was by no means a noisy Italian piazza, but nonetheless, encircled as it was by mature horse-chestnut trees, behind which were set a handful of buildings of architectural merit, including a forlorn savings bank and a forsaken church, the place had a distinctive pulse.

Morgan sat on a bench and stretched his arms along its back; he yawned and prompted by the prehibernal warmth surrendered himself to a light-heartedness and light-headedness of being. His eye was caught by a tiny, still nappied child who at that moment dropped its ball, watched it bounce, and, trying to catch it, stumbled, tripped over, lay prostrate for a moment then got up unhurt and went on playing. He continued to indulge his listless state simply observing the diverse shapes, sizes, ages and attire of the local population until the sun fell on the day and a chill crept into the air. He had made the right decision on how to honour his aunt and now he was pleased to return home where another letter was waiting for him. It was domestic not international, yet not official.

Turning it over to find the sender's name, he saw that

it was from the woman on the train, Lidiya K. His heart fluttered and he realised that he had been suppressing all thought of her in order to avoid disappointment. It was not a long letter, but neither was it just a note. In two pages she told him that when she had arrived home the house was as she had left it. At work, the director had unexpectedly resigned and one of her younger colleagues had in the space of a week divorced and remarried. She finished by expressing the hope that he had settled in and that when he had the time he would drop her a line to let her know whether the town was as she had described it. The overall tone of the letter seemed to him to display a droll, tongue-in-cheek sense of humour and a willingness to share with him aspects of her life which he thought were rather personal and quite intimate.

Morgan took two days to compose his reply. He had the first draft in his mind minutes after reading her letter. On paper though, the composition lacked refinement. Spontaneity yielded, as it so often does, to more cautious, time-consuming Deliberation. Even so, when he reached the point of popping the final version into the postbox, he couldn't quite dispel the thought that, despite his efforts, his pitch fell well short of being perfect.

Winter came: first the night frosts and ice-veneered puddles, then sleet and finally snow; after a brief testing of the ground, a great whiteness settled down and muffled the world. For long periods, blue skies and numbing temperatures gave everything the appearance and texturised feel of starched white linen; then the sky would turn into a steel-wool grey and the air would be full of gently fluttering flakes. Indoors Morgan wallowed in the tiled oven's swaddling warmth; outdoors, he crunched along paths trodden between glittering hillocks of snow.

Spring announced herself, slowly at first, then the icicles began to drip and collect in puddles; the snow on roofs melted and, as water, gurgled along gutters, poured down drain pipes, before finally gushing onto the pavements. With the days growing warmer, fresh buds courageously appeared on trees and people began to abandon their heavy overcoats for lighter ones. Later he recalled how it was on the very first day of setting off in the morning wearing just a jacket that he had received a telegram from Lidiya K. informing him that she would be arriving in two days' time on the overnight express from S. and that she would be staying for five days at no. 10 J-S Street.

The railway station was at the end of a boulevard of tall poplars. As Morgan approached the elaborately designed portal he had the nervous feeling he associated with the time he took his first Communion. He was brought down to earth from his reverie as soon as he pushed open the massive station door and collided with an old woman bowed under the weight of a heavy, sheet-draped bundle on her shoulder and a wicker basket of food in the crook of her arm. He apologised profusely and accepted her invective with a bowed head before rushing to check the scheduled and expected time of the train's arrival. He was neither surprised nor upset to find that it would be late, for it gave him time to relax and prepare himself for the materialisation of his fantasy.

Looking into the large, tarnished and distorting mirror behind the counter in the buffet, he recalled the hall of mirrors on the seaside pier at Cromer that bends the stature and deforms the features of those parading in front of it. Here the occupants of the room looked like a gathering of hobbits, many with bulbous noses and baggy trousers and mouths pulled into peculiar shapes by the cigarettes dripping off their lower lips. Even in mid-morning some of the transients and most of the habitués alike had already taken their places at the beer-wet counter. After nearly an hour, he gave a short sigh and, mumbling 'There but for the grace of God go I', finished drinking his lemon tea, paid and made his way to the platform to rehearse his body language and wait.

Since she had not told him the number of her carriage, he went to the end of the platform in the direction of the incoming train, so that she could see him as the train came into the station, for he was sure that she would be looking out for him. What, he wondered, did *he* want to be the first thing that she saw? Someone sitting, casually, on a porter's trolley reading? And, reading what? A book? A newspaper? Perhaps standing would be better. He practised different permutations, including ways of smiling as she descended from the carriage.

As it was a long train, the first four carriages glided

with hissing brakes past him quite quickly. He surmised that she would be in one of the sleepers. Those getting off were soon on the platform being embraced or walking alone to the exit, followed by the eyes of their former fellow passengers now leaning on the window curtain rail still in shirt sleeves and blouses.

The guard held up his tiny flag and blew his whistle, leaving Morgan to gaze along an almost totally deserted platform with a set of emotions fermenting on a spectrum ranging from disbelief and disappointment to frustration and irritation, verging on anger. As he watched the last carriage curve away from the station his state of agitation was chemically converted into a storm of self-pity, until he was rescued by an ego-defensive after-thought: he had not rehearsed for the scenario that he was now confronting. But before his lips could expand into a broad, self-mocking grin, a reflexive moment quietly pushed him to acknowledge the existence of the other person and ask himself, 'And what about her?'

The question prompted Guilt to gallop in to subdue his earlier egocentric reaction and refocus his emotional attention: Had something happened to prevent her catching the train? Had she been taken ill or been involved in an accident? His search for explanations extended to speculating that 'She must have missed the train', which in turn required a reason, such as 'because the taxi she had ordered was late' and so on. The flow of hypothetical causes and effects was amplified by other muddying tributaries: perhaps someone else, a close relative or friend, had been taken ill.

Morgan lingered on the platform for some time ruminating over and rearranging all his optional explanations for her not being on the train. Tellingly, every one of the reasons he put forward attributed her non-appearance in the play he'd scripted and on the stage he'd designed to some external factor. He never once contemplated the possibility that she had simply changed her mind.

As a result of his prolonged cogitation, it was already gone midday when he came out of the station, walked past the same beggars and back down the boulevard to the main road, intending to go home. Yet, on reaching the tram stop, he changed his mind and instead took a bus that went to that part of the town she had mentioned to him on several occasions both on the train and in their correspondence.

He'd been there twice: once soon after he'd settled in, as part of his purpose for being in the town, and again in the depth of the white winter in order to take photographs of the place she'd described as an overgrown village. As a result of these two forays he was relatively familiar with the neighbourhood and needed to ask only one person for directions to the actual street. The two-storeyed house where she had mentioned in her last letter that she would be staying was considerably larger than those immediately adjacent. Its decorative architraves had recently received a coat of pale blue paint and the porch running along the front of the house was wide enough for four people to sit at a table.

Receiving no reply to his knock on the door he went

down the side of the house, which was separated from its neighbour by a high, wobbly, wattle fence and found a middle-aged woman bent double tending a kitchen garden, as in a van Gogh sketch of aproned potato planters. He apologised for disturbing her and asked when she was expecting Ms K. to arrive. Pushing her hand on her hip, the woman slowly straightened her back. For a few moments the lips on her leathery and lined, drawn and drained face didn't move; instead, she narrowed her already squinting eyes, puckered her nose and deepened still further the furrows on her forehead ploughed by frowning.

'Who are you?' she eventually asked.

'I received a telegram from Ms K. telling me that she was arriving in town today and would be staying here, but I seem to have missed her at the station,' he said.

'Well, I don't know if she's coming or not. You can never tell with her; she changes her mind so easily,' the old woman offered gratuitously and testily.

Morgan paused, undecided what to say next; then he asked, 'Did she leave a message for me? My name is Morgan Davies.'

'No.' The answer was dispatched sharply and contemptuously through pursed lips. 'A letter in her handwriting arrived a few days ago but it's for someone else.' Although almost too sapped to speak, he managed to make a request: 'When she arrives, could you please tell her that I called?'

The old lady nodded her consent and he walked away. However, before he reached the gate, he stopped and turned back to the old woman now hoeing a row of carrots and said, 'I'm very sorry to have bothered you and, eh, you don't really need to say anything about my calling round. I'll contact her myself.'

His first steps away from the woman and the house – deliberate, long strides, shoulders back, head up, chin out – resembled the gait of a career soldier, a man in control of himself and the situation. By the end of the street, his whole mien had changed: both of his hands were dipped deep in his pockets, his shoulders slouched and his pace slowed. He dithered as though he had lost his way. All the questions he'd sifted and sorted at the station were again vying with one another for his attention, this time with those arising from what the old woman had told him.

Morgan's state of confusion didn't diminish during the bus ride home. He closed the door to his flat behind him, went into the small kitchen and switched on the kettle. Although as a self-imposed rule he never drank alcohol when unhappy or angry, now, he reached for a cognac glass on the top shelf and poured into it a small measure of the tawny liquid and, not for the first time in his life, adopted the part of Kean in Sartre's play of the same name: he twirled the short stem of the glass in his fingers, then cupped the bowl and sniffed the aroma before taking a small sip, which he swirled in his mouth before swallowing; he was consciously posturing as if he were an actor playing the role of a man wanting to assuage an acutely discomforting, but less than distressful, feeling.

Morgan put the empty glass down on the sill, walked away from the window, sat down at the table and opened the letter that he'd picked up off the floor when he had come into the house. Since his name and address were handwritten it could not be an official letter, yet the envelope had a local stamp.

The immediate effect of his association of a handwritten address with a local stamp was a quickening of his heartbeat in anticipation that his preferred explanation for the missing passenger was about to be confirmed. Instead, inside was another envelope with his name on it written in Charlie's idiosyncratic hand. As he had no interest in reading a letter from anyone but the woman on the train, his friend's spectral appearance immediately doused his briefly elevated spirit.

Charlie's previous letters recounted the professional ups and downs of their mutual friends, which he embellished with anecdotes of minor transgressions committed by one or two of them. The effect of these casual accounts and cheerful descriptions of life at home was sometimes to make Morgan smile, but just as frequently they upheld the scorn which he felt for the dull Lilliputian world from which he had temporarily escaped.

And yet, and yet, he thought to himself, folding his arms, and rocking back on the chair, Charlie's letters had another, reassuring aspect. In one way or another, they reaffirmed the world and way of life he knew. Now, lolling in the chair, he began to wonder whether that well-ordered world, which he was so keen to ridicule, possessed some merits, qualities to be appreciated as virtues rather than to be belittled as irredeemably flawed. He let the chair legs bang onto the floor and, deciding that this was not the time to join Alice and follow the white rabbit, he picked up his paper knife and deftly slit open the envelope in his hand.

Charlie began in his usual chirpy vein before slipping in, 'Here comes the difficult bit. I thought that I should prepare you for what *could* be bad news. I'm pretty sure that you can expect to hear from Janet fairly soon and she'll probably have some nasty things to say to you. She's found out about your affair in Vienna.'

Morgan's mouth dropped and a muffled 'Oh, no' staggered out of it in a comic strip bubble.

'I've often wondered just how long you'd be able to keep that a secret,' Charlie added, echoing Morgan's intermittent fear, then continued, 'According to one of Janet's friends, she's had a couple of sessions with a counsellor, but when I saw her, which was after she'd got to know about Astrid, she didn't mention her to me or say anything about your marriage being over, but then I'm your friend. On the other hand, I have heard that she's talked in these terms to someone else.' Charlie then went into philosophical mode, which seamlessly drifted into mentioning affairs involving high status, though non-celebrity, couples who had managed to weather the storm and stay together.

Morgan tucked Charlie's palliative words away to

replay later. He put the letter down, slumped into the worn armchair and stared into space. As his vitality ebbed away, nervous stress, physical exhaustion and ethanol combined to summon Morpheus to bring deep sleep and a reconciling dream.

When he opened his eyes it was dusk and the temperature had fallen. Since the dream was still fresh and vivid, he dropped his shutters again and rewound the film in order to imprint the narrative in his memory. After a few minutes, feeling slightly refreshed, he pushed himself up and walked to the window to draw the curtains. In his interpretation of the dream, Janet was unmistakably the central figure. He went to the sink, refilled the kettle and sat down at the kitchen table to write three letters, dreading, not just suspecting, that not one would strike the right note.

3

Penultimate Skirmish

It was late afternoon on just another Thursday. As it happens, if you must know, it was in June, though it could have been January. The telephone rang in the lounge and a voice immediately rang out from the bedroom. 'Lawrence! The phone's ringing. Why don't you pick it up?'

To an outsider, the woman's hoarse voice would have sounded angry. To the person being addressed the loud and piercing cry was quite normal; nevertheless, even though habituated to its tone, the rasp of this former heavy Gauloises smoker never ceased to grate on him and, as now, caused him to wince.

'My hands are full,' he replied in a voice that he knew would be audible to the person upstairs. He never raised his voice to match the imperious quality of the other because he knew for certain that to do so, justifiably or not, would be damagingly counterproductive. Exercising self-control paid him an enormous dividend: inner peace and minimal external aggression.

'Then drop whatever it is, I'm expecting a new member of my women's group to call,' the voice commanded.

'*My* group,' he muttered to himself and then said aloud, 'I told you, my hands are full. I'm carrying the present that you bought yesterday; the one you wanted to take to your bridge club this evening.'

'Oh, well, in that case, put the present down gently somewhere, since, as you well know, it's very fragile.' The voice was momentarily calmer. But with the next sentence a reprehending harshness returned. 'Pick up the phone,' she cried out, just as it stopped ringing. 'You are the limit. You know that I'm trying to get dressed and I'm late.'

'What's her name if she rings again?'

'Antonia,' came the terse reply.

'Our Antonia should be pleased to meet another one.'

'Don't be facetious, please, Lawrence.'

At the time when he'd been summoned by phone and voice, Lawrence was wearing a pair of slightly worn, brownish-yellow cords and a cream, broad-checked, short-sleeved shirt – his gardening clothes. Now, getting on in years, he was no more stooped than the average man of his age and boasted a good head of light grey hair that would soon turn silver. His blue eyes permanently twinkled over cheeks reddened by wine and above parted lips ever waiting to tell a joke, recount an anecdote or respond with a witty or quizzical riposte to a comment made by someone else at the table – in the restaurant, at home, around the pool, at the beach or golf club.

He had not long settled into an armchair to watch a live broadcast of a cricket Test match when a short, stout, overweight and over-made-up woman came into the room. She was wearing a long black dress sprinkled with silvery sequins and with lace around the chest and arms, all set off by a heavy gold necklace. The rings on three fingers on each hand were combinations of gold and platinum, each studded with emeralds, sapphires or diamonds. She stretched out her arm to examine with her fox-like eyes her varnished digits, which taken together looked like a bling knuckleduster.

'You really shouldn't be smoking so much, Lawrence,' she said, shaking her head, as he took a drag and passed it to her. She declined by shaking her head then took it from him, inhaled deeply and handed it back.

'You shouldn't drink so much,' he replied without looking at her, instead groaning as the ball sent a stump flying into the air.

'You're a fine one to talk. Anyway, are you or aren't you going to drive me over to Frida's?'

'I'd rather not. But I'll get your car out for you, if you like. I mean, you don't expect me to sit around with your cackling crowd, twiddling my fingers while you play cards all evening and then drive you home? Do you? Yes, you do.'

'Alright, but don't expect me always to come to the

hospital with you and hold your hand. You've got an appointment tomorrow. You'd forgotten, hadn't you?'

'I know I have an appointment. I hadn't forgotten. And that's more reason for me to rest quietly here rather than dash all the way over there. You seem to forget that rushing around raises my blood pressure.'

'Oh, Lawrence, for God's sake. You and your bloody blood pressure and other ailments. Why don't you bear them in silence like I do mine?'

'You! Bear your ailments in silence? Is that what you tell your new psychiatrist? That you never complain about your aches and pains?'

'Let's not go there, please. I should never have told you that I had decided to see a psychiatrist.' Dorothea paused and then added, 'You know full well that I went to see him because of you. I don't mean because of what you do to me, well, not directly. I had asked Sheila from International House... You know whom I'm talking about, don't you, dear?' She turned her head to one side, looking at him with a sardonic Cheshire cat smile and only just managing to refrain from patting his head. 'Well, never mind, dear. Let me remind you. I explained to her – Sheila that is – that I needed to talk to someone – not any old person, but someone who knew their stuff; someone with a good reputation. I didn't want to see one of these half-baked so-called therapists. Bloody charlatans most of them. You know very well that I don't like opening myself up to anyone at all, so I was determined that I would only lay myself bare...'

'Not a pleasant sight...'

'For Christ's sake Lawrence, shut up!'

'Just joking,' Lawrence said with a pursed-lip grin.

'As I was saying I would only go to see a consultant who was not only strongly recommended, but came with the most impeccable credentials.'

'As you always do, Dotty. And quite right too. You deserve the best. Only someone of the highest calibre,' Lawrence said quietly without lifting his eyes from the screen.

'I can do without your sarcasm, if you don't mind. I wanted the best so that I could better understand you and help *you*. I don't need someone *for me*, but *for you*.' She gave another beaming smile – the sort that social workers give to individuals in their case load whom they have classified as 'confused elderly'.

'Don't forget that you're paying for this out of my pension,' Lawrence couldn't stop himself from saying.

'I beg your pardon! This comes out of my pension, if you don't mind,' Dorothea blustered.

'Let's drop it, shall we. Of course, it's your money that you're spending.'

'Thank you for recognising that, Lawrence, so, I agree, let's not mention the matter any further.'

Anyone watching this exchange and with no knowledge of the couple would have had difficulty deciphering his smile; either Lawrence was indeed demented or he was totally *compos mentis* and merely deferring to the explanation given by the person who was almost literally his life-long companion, to whose fallibilities and frailties he had grown accustomed. After so many years together, the strong feelings towards the mannerisms and attributes they disliked in each other had largely dissipated.

According to Lawrence's philosophy of life, which in a nutshell concerned his self-preservation, arguing with Dorothea at their age simply wasn't worth the candle. Discussing out of whose budget the psychiatrist was being paid would serve no purpose unless he wanted to antagonise her. Furthermore, he could see no benefit from pointing out that he knew full well that Dorothea was seeing a psychiatrist for herself. Moreover, this particular topic was one on which he preferred to remain silent because there was more than an outside chance that he might turn out to be the main beneficiary of her spending yet more money on being pampered by another oracle.

Dorothea drove herself the ten miles to the home of the group member who was hosting the evening's game of bridge, where she would chat, gossip, eat and drink and be social and try very hard to win. Dorothea did not play with her usual partner, who had informed the hostess earlier in the week that a simmering family matter had suddenly boiled over and she had been called upon to go and mediate in order to avoid an expensive litigation. Everyone had accepted Natalie's apologies as genuine, except Dorothea, whose misgivings essentially derived from the fact that Nats had not contacted her directly and apologised in person. In the event, although Dorothea and her temporary partner had played well together, by the end of the evening they had come fourth in the final tally. The faint praise that she bestowed on her partner wasn't enough to muffle her grumble about having been let down by Natalie's unfortunate absence.

Since Dorothea always kept the group up to date on Lawrence's hospital tests, diagnoses and prognoses, each of the players had asked after him. 'He's such good fun,' Lucy had said. 'Yes, he's one of those lovely men who always has a joke up his sleeve and a smile on his face,' Jane had added.

'Not if you live with him,' Dorothea blurted out with a stony-faced look.

'Still, I bet he's much better than my old man,' said Lucy.

'What are you saying?' Frida asked. 'Your Hector may not be the life and soul of a party but, come on, he pulls his weight.'

'I suppose you're right, he's not that bad really,' Lucy conceded before turning to Dorothea and saying, 'But you don't know just how lucky you are Dotty to have a man like Lawrence.' Lucy's praise for her husband was one that Dorothea preferred not to hear, for in her opinion she had to put up far more with Lawrence than they did with their husbands. What's more, it was Lawrence who was the lucky one for having her to care for him.

The conversation around the table before and after the game briefly engaged with parochial politics and grander

European-wide issues before settling down into a burble about quotidian stuff, including the maladies of their adult children, their husbands and partners and various step-relations, before focusing on their own physical infirmities and the failing faculties of their spouses.

One or two of them were characteristically less forthcoming about themselves, but most were unable to conceal their self-absorption – least of all Dorothea; she recounted in great detail her own health problems and accidents, virtually all of which, barring a few of her sicknesses, she forcefully insisted were entirely attributable to the negligence of others.

Each of her ailments was delivered as a droning monologue to an audience which either listened with bowed heads in silence or looked on with eyes as glazed as cherries in a fruitcake. They only came awake when Dorothea had finished talking about herself and turned to finish apprising them of Lawrence's situation. Her monochrome description of the advice and prescriptions he had received from his different consultants – which were cursorily dismissed with a wave of the hand – contrasted with the vivid technicolour representation she gave of her own cinematographic biopic. To this post-bridge audience, the scale of Dorothea's infirmities fell into the category of being 'epic', while Lawrence's were categorised as a lightly entertaining, supporting 'short' to the main drama in her household.

When she had finished, Frida said, 'Dorothea, you speak as if Lawrence's medical problems aren't as grave as the consultants are saying.'

'I didn't say that. What I said is that Lawrence believes that his health is worse than I think it is.'

'Yes, but, does he think that his health is worse than that identified by the consultants?'

'I didn't say that either.'

There was a pause then Maria, Dorothea's partner for the evening, stood up, went to fetch a bottle of water and, willing to risk being the butt of Dorothea's easily aroused sense of self-righteous indignation, said over her shoulder, 'Aren't you worried about Lawrence's health, Dorothea? I mean, I know that you're worried about him if he's not well, but is it that you think that his problems are being exaggerated either by him or by his specialists?'

Dorothea looked from one person to another and then raised her head and jutted out her Habsburg-like jaw as if she were to make a regal pronouncement: 'I *am* worried about Lawrence's health. Of course I am. And I look after him and make sure he goes to the hospital when he has an appointment. But, yes, I think that his consultants, like all consultants, overstate the extent of the illness. In other words, again, yes, I do believe that Lawrence's complaint is not as serious as they would like us to believe.'

★

Lawrence was pleased to be alone. He had watched the Test match to the close of play, listened to the news on four different channels, eaten a simple meal, consumed the greater part of a bottle of red wine and read the newspaper. On a couple of occasions he had strained his ears to listen for any unusual sound because he was unable to completely push out of his mind that they had now been burgled three times, most recently just two months ago, when both he and Dorothea had been in the house. Antonia, the old, partially deaf, mixed parentage, Dachshund-shaped golden Retriever had not barked because the intruders had the nous to sedate her.

None of these diversions – the match, news or burglary – could completely distract him from the agonising pain in his left shoulder for which he was under constant surveillance by different hospital specialists. The consultant in whom he had most faith was recommending surgery. However, because opinion was divided over the diagnosis, agreement could not be reached on the best course of treatment.

Having managed to stay awake, when he heard the electronically controlled gate roll open and the distinctive sound of Dorothea's car come up the gravel drive, he hauled himself up out of his armchair and unlocked the door to greet her. As she puffed up the steps, her first words were: 'It was a bloody dreadful evening. God knows why they had to choose Maria to be my partner for the evening.'

'May I assume, my beloved, that you lost again?' Lawrence quizzed.

'Yes. We didn't win. Does that make you feel better?'

'I was only asking.'

'But why did you say "again"?'

'I shouldn't have added the adverb.'

'You're right there. You shouldn't have bloody well asked. When you lose at golf, I don't say, "So, you lost again", do I?'

'That's true, Dotty, but then you're almost always on the course in your buggy to see how well or badly I've played.'

'Is that relevant?'

'Whether it is or whether it isn't, it's time for bed.'

'I agree. We have an early appointment with your doctor tomorrow.'

Despite having taken alongside his usual tramadol an extra paracetamol before pulling himself up the stairs, Lawrence had slept badly and was now up earlier than usual. He went into the farmhouse-style kitchen and pressed the button on the mechanically controlled shutter which, when retracted, revealed a cloudless, spirit-uplifting, post-dawn sky.

By seven o'clock he had completed his ablutions and had eaten his normal modest breakfast. At seven-thirty he went back up the stairs to wake his wife. He felt certain that today he would have to take a critical, life-affecting decision. Both he and the principal consultant – whom he had an appointment to see in two hours' time – had more or less agreed that the next time they met Lawrence would have to make up his mind one way or the other. By then the consultant would have discussed his case again with the two other specialists who were knowledgeable about his syndrome.

While grateful for the attention he'd received from all three of them, each an expert in his narrow field, Lawrence harboured, quite uncharacteristically, a smouldering grievance; he did not understand why the three wise men had not once met up together with him to discuss their individual diagnoses and prescriptions for action.

From the moment she'd come downstairs Dorothea jabbered almost non-stop until they reached their destination. She referred to his pain, the apparently contrasting diagnoses that had been made not just by the current consultants but by previous specialists, and went into detail about her disdain for consultants in general: she disliked the way they dressed (the colourful Swatch watch, for example), how they looked and spoke; she found fault with their personal mannerisms – a twitch of the lip, the lifting of the eyebrow suggesting curiosity, the inauthentic frown and the twirling of the thumbs or stumpy Montblanc fountain pen. They all irritated her.

Most of her conversation, however, concerned people in their domestic and social lives who, in her eyes, were not doing their jobs properly: the gardener, the builder, the lawyer, even the butcher for the poor quality of the meat he sold to them for their consumption and which he set aside for poor, ailing Antonia.

As they approached the clinic, Dorothea stopped talking and just looked straight ahead at the oasis of health. This gave Lawrence an opportunity to express his own anxiety. 'You know, Dotty, I think that they would like to operate, but having examined my angiogram and MRI scans they might be too worried to do so.'

'Oh, Lawrence, don't be so stupid!' Dorothea scolded him with a scowl. And then, as if to cover herself against any future mishap, repeated her admonition: 'I've been telling you for years to cut down on your smoking.' Nevertheless, Lawrence's melancholic and portentous utterance had been chastening.

The private clinic was situated in its own grounds outside the town and near a spa complex. For Lawrence, who described himself as having come into the world a natural sceptic and who was going to depart as a healthy dystopian cynic, it made perfect sense for the private equity group that had invested in the clinic to incorporate into its business plan the construction of a more or less adjacent spa.

Lawrence parked the car in a space just metres from the entrance. They walked through revolving glass doors into an air-conditioned atrium, the centrepiece of which was a marble fountain topped by a replica of the Peloponnesian statue of Asclepius posing with his serpent-entwined staff.

The terracotta-tiled floor was interspersed with skilfully crafted copies of fragments of Sicilian mosaics from the Villa Romana del Casale, and a variety of urns and amphora of different sizes; some of these were painted and upright and others tilted on their side; some were filled with leafy plants. The vases had been selected by the award-winning team of architects, commissioned by the investors, because of the sensuousness of rounded shapes; the urns, originally created to hold the necessities of life, were the symbolic embodiment of the building's purpose, which was to hold and warmly embrace the people who came to be healed.

These feminine shapes stood or lay amongst a few fluted half columns, behind which had been artfully placed a subliminally detectable, slyly smiling cherubic head. (The inclusion of the latter had been the subject of intense argument amongst the architects themselves and of more muted discussion with the client.) The aesthetic and overall ambience, combined with quietly flowing water and piped birdsong, was intended to lull the customer-patients into a sense of the well-being enjoyed by privileged groups during what is known as 'classical antiquity'.

When Dorothea and Lawrence entered this space they found only two other people: the receptionist, who stood as they entered, and a man in his early middle age sitting in a comfortable-looking chair and leafing through a magazine. The foyer was not a waiting room, for none of the visitors ever waited; they were paying large sums of money in order not to do so.

'Good morning, madam,' the Colgate-advertising receptionist said to Dorothea who walked ahead of Lawrence. 'You've a 9.30 appointment with Mr Charles.'

'I know that,' said Dorothea looking the breezy thirty

year old in the eye, supplementing her gruff reply with 'and we're on time, as usual.'

'Yes, of course. Mr Charles will see you immediately.'

As if on cue a good-looking man in his early forties, well-tanned and lean, dressed in designer slacks, a monogrammed shirt and soft, polished and tasselled moccasin-styled shoes came towards them, addressing Dorothea first of all. 'Nice to see you again, Mrs Faraway.'

'It's Faraday,' said Lawrence.

'I know. Of course. I'm so sorry. Please forgive me. It's a bit of a cliché but I'm dreadful with names – of people that is, not diagnoses and treatments.' He gave a little chuckle at his joke and led them down a short corridor and into a spacious consulting room.

'You do it on purpose, don't you?' said Dorothea trying to keep up with him. 'It's not the first time. Have you ever called Lawrence "Mr Faraway"?'

'Dotty, please. Be quiet, just for a little while until we're back in the car,' Lawrence said shaking his head and letting his mouth droop like a tired old spaniel.

Daniel Charles heard and ignored her question. He recalled that the husband had made the same plea to his wife on previous occasions when he had met them together. Besides having an established reputation as one of the best neurosurgeons in the region, with a visiting professorship in a top teaching hospital, Daniel Charles liked to think that he was a good psychologist. He enjoyed trying to penetrate the state of mind of his patients and to speculate about them as individuals and about their relationships with other people; attempting to dissect the odd mind could be more challenging and pleasurable than taking the scalpel to their bodies.

He pushed the door and held it open to allow Dorothea and Lawrence to cross the threshold into a space more like the lounge of an English gentlemen's club than a consulting room. What linked it, in architectural conception, to the foyer-atrium was Classicism with its sense of harmony and idealism. Although the clinic was obviously neither a spa nor a boutique hotel, for those who used these facilities all three of them were designed to be used by individuals wealthy enough to pay for the privilege of being there.

The consultancy room had a polished, light walnut floor, around one-third of which was further brightened by Persian rugs. Two of the walls were decoratively protected by tall, but not ceiling high, bookcases punctuated either by ornately and gilt-framed portraits of patrons or individuals who had contributed to the advancement of medical knowledge, or by similarly framed paintings of mythical and pastoral scenes. Mr Charles was able, if requested, to elaborate at length on the provenance and significance of every painting in the room and explain its connection to the clinic.

Inside the room, off centre, was a coffee table appropriate in height to the seating which consisted of four low armchairs upholstered in dominantly blue ottoman silk. Further away towards the window was a large, deep green, leather-topped writing desk made from briar root, whose legs and side drawers were embellished with delicate motifs and engravings; its top was entirely bare apart from a couple of neatly tied folders, a desk diary, an inkwell, two pens and a pencil.

'Mrs Far…'

'Faraday,' Dorothea jumped in.

'Mrs Faraday,' Mr Charles continued, giving Dorothea a wan smile, 'would you like to sit here?' moving a chair towards her by a fraction.

'No. I'd prefer to sit on this one, if you don't mind.'

'Not at all,' Daniel said with a barely perceptible shrug.

'There's no need to shrug. We're paying you good money. And we're only doing that because we have it on good authority that you are the best person in the field as far as my husband's problem is concerned. In this country, that is.'

'Thank you for the compliment,' the already eminent surgeon said, restraining himself from adding, 'and beyond the borders of this country'.

Lawrence, his head bowed, looked both sheepish and peeved. He was in pain and was concerned about his health. He did not want to have to cope with another tantrum and more unseemly behaviour on the part of his wife. 'Dotty, stop being so discourteous. We've come to listen to what Mr Charles has to say. I want to know what he thinks should be done.'

Dorothea looked into the tunnel between her husband and one of society's high priests, whose diagnosis and prognosis might turn out to be the modern medical equivalent of giving extreme unction. Lawrence, who was bending forward with his hands on his knees, looked up and tilted his head. His posture reflected his state of ambiguity: should he make light of the situation and tell a joke or look solemn and grave? He decided on the Hollywood cowboy cliché: 'Give it to me, doc,' he said squinting and winking at the consultant as though they were partners in a revue.

Daniel Charles winked back and moving his head slowly from side to side said, 'I sure will, Larry. I cannot tell a lie. I never could. Because if I did, I just wouldn't sleep right.'

'Stop fooling around the two of you,' Dorothea interjected.

Mr Charles cleared his throat, ran his fingers through his hair and continued: 'Well, I've consulted my colleagues here in the clinic, all of whom you've seen for other health-related matters and who are very familiar with your medical history. I've also spoken to one of the research teams at the university who, I am pleased to be able to tell you, are on the brink of a breakthrough in understanding the causes of your particular problem. On the basis of the results from your most recent tests, the details that we have of your medical history and of this latest research we, that is, I, have come to the decision that you have a choice...'

'What the hell do you mean, "choice"? We, I mean, my husband here, doesn't want to make a choice. That's your job. You're the professional, sun-tanned professor. You're the one who should be making a decision,' Dorothea shouted.

'Dotty, shut up!' Lawrence said glaring at her.

'Don't you tell me to shut up. It shouldn't be left to

us to make choices,' she yelled, jabbing the air with her forefinger. 'Their job is to look at all the results and all the information at their disposal about your condition, then make an assessment, arrive at a judgement and tell us their recommendation.'

'And that, Mrs Faraday, is precisely why we're meeting today. I can and shall make a recommendation based on the evidence available to us. It is then for Mr Faraday to make a decision.'

Dorothea's eyes were darting everywhere. She didn't really want to hear his proposal for action and was mentally prepared to contradict and refute whatever he proposed.

'We are now certain that we know what is causing Lawrence so much pain and why the treatments and palliatives that we have tried over the past three months have not succeeded in alleviating it. We are equally sure that surgery would solve the problem.'

'That's what we thought all along,' Dorothea said glowering at the consultant. 'I don't know why you didn't do that in the first place instead of doing this and that while poor Lawrence has been in agony. And, let me tell you, I know what agony is and I know the agony that he has been going through,' Dorothea added in a more subdued and empathetic voice.

'How long would the operation take?' Lawrence asked, aware that this was not the most important question in the queue waiting to be asked.

'Oh, not long at all. About ninety minutes. Maybe two hours. It's very straightforward.'

'Then why didn't you do this a long time ago?' Dorothea pushed.

'Because we wanted to avoid surgery if possible, even though we thought that, in the end, if Mr Faraday's problem was to be resolved, surgery would be required.'

'You're talking a lot of bollocks if you don't mind me saying so. I've got a good mind to sue you for negligence,' Dorothea blustered.

'Dotty, if you don't keep quiet, then I think that you should leave the room. I'll discuss Mr Charles's recommendation with him and let you know afterwards,' Lawrence said firmly but calmly. The last thing that he wanted was for him or Mr Charles to put a torch to his wife's ever brimful tank of truculence.

Mr Charles poured them each a glass of water from a decanter and then said more solemnly, 'There is only one major issue and this explains why we have pursued other paths before returning to surgery.' Then, addressing himself directly to Lawrence, he added, 'You have smoked so heavily for so many years that your heart is not as strong as we would like it to be for you to have a full anaesthetic. In other words, having surgery to remedy your problem comes with a risk.'

'What a filthy trick!' Dorothea screamed and threw the glass as hard as she could on the floor smashing it.

'Just shut up, Dotty, and get out. I have a choice: either I continue to live with the pain or risk having surgery from which I may not recover. That's straightforward enough. It's my choice.' Lawrence's eyes moved between his wife and the consultant. It was indeed his choice: an excruciatingly painful existence or the risk of dying.

'I'd like to correct you there, my boy,' Dorothea screamed as she stood up and walked towards the book case where she began to take books out of their ordered shelves and in a controlled way throw them one by one in all directions. 'I'm part of this "choice", as you call it. I have a say in all this too, not just you two men!' she shouted at the top of her voice.

'Of course, you do, Dotty,' said Lawrence conciliatorily. In order to reduce his rising anxiety, behind his every thought and gesture was his determination to placate his wife. Although this was hardly the first time that she had thrown a tantrum in public, he had never personally witnessed such extreme and unwarranted behaviour.

Moreover, usually his embarrassment at her displays of irascibility was reduced by the fact that they occurred when they were amongst friends and acquaintances, whose numbers, incidentally, had dwindled in recent years because of these outbursts.

'Your husband is quite right. It goes without saying that you have to be involved in any decision which affects both your lives. The choice isn't an easy one,' Daniel Charles said piously with a little crinkling of the forehead.

Dorothea's mouth dropped open and her jaw moved up and down, her eyes glazing over momentarily; her arms flailed about as though she was thrashing out at invisible people and she tottered over to another chair into which she dropped her corpulent body; she sat there with her head tilted back, sucking in air in a series of gasps. Lawrence and Daniel sat immobilised in shock; unlike the poor inhabitants of Pompeii they were only temporarily suffocated by the fall-out from Dorothea's Vesuvian explosion.

Then she heaved herself up and bellowed, 'You bloody useless tossers! Excuse my French. There is no choice?!' She then made her way back to the bookshelves and again started to wrench books off them.

Her first assault on the condensed thoughts of the cleverest human beings of their generation had been an unpremeditated rehearsal for the fury which she now unleashed on this miniature of the polite society to which she always averred that she belonged.

'Are you telling us that the only thing that all these damned, supposedly learned, books can tell you, and then for you to tell us, is, "You can either put up with your unbearable pain or risk death under the scalpel"? A witchdoctor could probably offer better options!'

Before the two men could stop her Dorothea was hurling books in all directions: at them, at glass cabinets, at busts on pedestals and reclining Etruscan figurines on a Louis Quatorze cabinet. Lawrence was the first to make a move to restrain her from continuing her rampage. He wrapped his arms around her and attempted to wrestle her towards a chaise longue.

'Come on, Dotty. Calm down. What the hell's got into you? I've never seen you like this before. What's wrong? Tell me.'

Dorothea's response was to let loose a torrent

of invective: 'Bugger off, you stupid bastard. You let everyone just walk all over you. Well, no one's walking over me!' she screamed at the top of her voice. Her scream seemed to generate enough energy to break away from his hold. Without saying a word, the much younger and stronger Mr Charles, who had pressed a security button on his desk, now enveloped her in a powerful embrace. He had only been holding her for seconds before the door opened and two security assistants with paramedical training came in. While one took over holding Dorothea, the other produced a syringe and injected Dorothea in the arm.

It had been such a blisteringly hot summer that water restrictions had been imposed in the local area. However, the clinic was not affected so that when Daniel Charles and Lawrence Faraday came through the revolving door, the little stream was still gurgling, its refreshing sound replenishing and settling the spirits of visitors.

With his arm drooped over Lawrence's shoulder, Mr Charles steered him towards his consulting room.

'Something to quench the thirst, apart from water?' Daniel asked.

'No. Not in this heat, especially at this time of day, thank you,' Lawrence replied and, not waiting to be invited, sat down in what was now his customary chair.

'So, in retrospect my malapropism of referring to Dorothea as Mrs Far-away was, quite by chance, almost an accurate name for her. I don't want to joke at her expense, but don't you think that one can't help smiling at the fact that, towards the end of her life, your wife has come to live up to her shortened familiar name, Dotty?' said Mr Charles squeezing his patient's shoulder.

'You're right except for one thing: she has spent much of her life, not just the end of it, living up to her familiar name. You know, she was never "Dot" and would be quite rude to anyone who called her that. But she wasn't dotty in the sense of being harmlessly eccentric. She was odd, you know, peculiar – words she often used to describe other people – and outlandish.' Lawrence paused and Mr Charles chose not to fill the space, preferring to grant his patient the time he needed to find the right words.

'The term that best captures her behaviour is "outrageous". To say that she was immoderate would be an understatement; she took offence very easily and could flare up at the drop of a hat and then become violent, although, I have to say, never as bad as on that occasion – the one you witnessed. I don't like to say it, but at times she could be quite cruel towards a person directly to their face or about them in their absence.'

Lawrence paused once more and the consultant again decided to remain silent to allow his elderly patient time to reminisce and find other words to describe his spouse of fifty years. After less than a minute's silence, he leaned forward and put his hands on his knees and looked up into the eyes of his doctor. He held his gaze for a few seconds, smiled and looked down at his hands.

Noticing that Lawrence's eyes were moistening, Daniel Charles changed hats and in his role as amateur psychologist asked, 'Did you have a nickname at school which you carried with you like Dorothea did?'

'Ha ha, you'd never guess,' chuckled Lawrence. 'It was 'Lolly' or 'Lol' before the name became an internet acronym.'

'Lol? I haven't heard it used,' Daniel confessed with a shake of the head. 'All the same, Dotty and Lolly,' he said, glancing at his watch and beginning to stand up, still laughing and nodding his head at the irony. 'It's time to go and see old Dotty. We can come back here afterwards to finish our conversation and make that decision which we keep postponing.'

Dorothea was partially sitting up in a bed in the private wing of a nearby hospital. Little teardrops dripped from her reddened eyes. Her lips opened and shut like a goldfish in a bowl. Daniel Charles was standing beside her; he had taken a personal interest in Dorothea largely because it was the first time in his life that he had observed such a paroxysm caused by someone in the throes of a mental breakdown. Lawrence was sitting on a chair behind him and just outside Dorothea's field of vision. 'What is she saying?' he asked.

'She's barely audible,' said Daniel, 'but she seems to be repeating the same thing over and over again.'

'And?' Lawrence asked.

'It sounds to me that she keeps muttering the same words: "Mummy, Mummy, please don't leave me. I need you. You're too young to die."'

'Oh, no. Really! Are you sure? My hearing's not so good. She could be saying "Bob's your uncle" which for some peculiar reason is one of her favourite expressions. I never knew why she used it. And I never asked her why she did. Perhaps she had a crush on an uncle called Bob.' Lawrence gave a little chuckle and then taking a deep breath he looked Mr Charles in the eye and said in a more serious tone:

'It's a funny thing, Daniel, but when you're first in love with a person you ask them to disclose all sorts of things about themselves. Why they do this, why they do that, why they believe this and why they say that. If those questions aren't asked in the first year or, at a guess five years, they'll never be asked. That's why, even after living with someone for fifty years, there's a lot of simple things you don't understand about them because you never asked. So, beware, young man.'

'I'll remember that, Lawrence. Thank you. As to your question: yes, those are the words that she has been repeating for some time.'

'How fascinating. But I shouldn't be surprised,' said Lawrence. 'It's true, her mother did die quite young. Of cancer. So do you think that's the reason for – what should we call it? – her breakdown? She still misses her mother?'

'I don't think that that's the reason, although it would be worthwhile seeking the opinion of her psychiatrist.'

'That's a good idea. It would be nice to have an explanation. But, if it's not her mother's death, Mr Charles, what do you think was the cause?'

'Let's go back to my room where we can talk about that as well as finish off our main business. But, as we walk over there, I leave you to ponder the idea that it's not the death of someone she was most attached to over half a century ago but the possible death of someone to whom she's been attached for an equally lengthy period of time.'

'Can I get you a drink, Lawrence?' Daniel Charles asked once they were sitting down again.

'More water, please. And, given the hour, could I have a spritzer?'

'Of course you can. Anything you like.' Daniel went to his desk, placed the order and by the time he had flicked through a folder, the receptionist had brought in their drinks – two glasses of iced water and lemon, one spritzer and a coffee – and put them on the table.

Daniel Charles sat down and stretched his legs out in front of him. He locked his long, manicured fingers and bowed his head down towards Lawrence. 'Look. We could talk about Dorothea all day, so let's deal with you first. After all, we met because of you. You're my priority. What have you decided? Not an easy decision, but at least you've had plenty of time to think and weigh up the different options and the risks.'

Lawrence, in an exaggerated imitation of the consultant, cocked his head, hunched his shoulders and, giving Daniel a sidelong glance with a half-closed, conspiratorial eye, said, 'I'll go for the operation, doc.'

4

Thuggery in the Public Interest

It wasn't the first time. Far from it. And yet, it always caused him anxiety. He switched on and while he waited checked his diary just to make sure that he knew the choices open to him. Realising that he had left little time for manoeuvre, he became annoyed with himself; there had been no need to procrastinate as he had done; now he would have to choose quickly before it became prohibitively expensive. Then, as soon as he had made up his mind on which flight to take, the whole process of booking online was quickly completed. He slept well with his mind at rest, since he would be in Helsinki for the opening session. Two days later he was on his way.

As he walked towards the Tube station he saw a crowd of tribally dressed youths – 'yooff,' he said to himself moving his lips but emitting scarcely a breath of sound. To someone more generous they were just a group of boisterous, high-spirited young men. To him, though, they were noisy and rowdy. Their scarves and bobble hats were in the colours of the local football team. No doubt they were off to watch a match, either from the terraces or on the big screen in a pub. Afterwards, with their tanks full they would be fuelled to cheer as victors or curse as the defeated. A few of the more exuberant amongst them would transmogrify into riotous hooligans, most of whom, when they later appeared before the magistrates, would be given small fines or have their cases dismissed. A tiny minority would already be well known to the members of the bench who informally and noiselessly (like one of the triumvirate of wise monkeys) would brand them as a bunch of thugs.

Descending in the empty lift to the Underground platform Sebastian muttered the word 'thug' out loud: 'Thug. A member of a group of people who practise thuggery.' The word, he recalled, comes from the Hindi *'thuggee'*. This was the name for a semi-religious Hindu cult with a highly organised system of murder and robbery, which like *suttee* (the obligatory self-immolation of a wife on the funeral pyre of her dead husband) was abolished by the British early in their nineteenth-century suzerainty of India.

It was highly likely, he mused, that these historical facts learned from his schoolboy history textbook, imprinted in his memory and on which he had been examined, would by now have been challenged by anti-colonialists somewhere in the world; their contestation would centre on condemning the manner in which *thuggee* and *suttee*, for example, were reported rather than the acts themselves. They'd use terms such as 'moral panics' to underplay the cruelty of these groups and their customs; instead of abhorring these practices for what they were, these critics of the European colonial powers would probably argue that the British authorities gained from inflating their significance; their intervention to outlaw these indigenous conventions was a means of justifying their presence in India and their consolidation of power; it allowed them to hold up their actions as evidence of the beneficence of their civilising rule.

For the post-modern historiographer, including post-imperial historians, while our understanding of past cults, such as *thuggee* and *suttee*, is advanced by seeing and interpreting them from different standpoints, there is a lurking danger in doing so: accentuating the need to take a sympathetic account of these traditions and customs from the position of those within the local society can unintentionally encourage an amoral cultural relativism.

The onomatopoeic sound of the word 'thug' probably facilitated its transfer into English usage for it accurately describes and labels behaviour that is regarded as nasty as well as violent. According to current Anglophone convention, to say that a person's behaviour is 'thuggish' carries with it a strong moral connotation, making it worse than an act defined simply as 'criminal'. Depending on the nature of the crime and often the social class of its perpetrator, an individual charged with an offence against a person rather than property is likely to be condemned by the media and the judiciary for having committed a 'thuggish' crime.

The name has also been used to describe individuals

and groups struggling for elbow room and influence in the political arena. Apart from its sarcastic use to portray the odd, physically or verbally pugnacious, mainstream Parliamentarian, it has mainly been applied to members of groups located at the extreme wings of the political spectrum: 'communist thugs' and 'fascist thugs'. From a centrist point of view, generally speaking, the former have been seen as less pernicious than the latter because they at least were internationalist and forward looking – whatever that really means – while the fascist variety are nationalist and backwards looking. With the confinement of communism to the occasional cloistered cell, the thuggish, extreme left-wing element within the British political system has, by the beginning of the twenty-first century, largely, but not entirely, withered away. The same may not be said of the fascistic extreme which has been witnessing a revival.

'The point is…' Sebastian almost said aloud, '"fascist" is not a term to be used loosely and applied willy-nilly to anyone expressing views regarded as 'unacceptable' by individuals inhabiting political territory left of centre. Who, he pondered, is the more dangerous: the person who privately expresses right-wing opinions and harbours authoritarian attitudes and is a member of an extreme right-wing political group or a state official employed to 'weed out enemies of the people'? Would it not be more apt to attach the label 'fascist thug' to individuals who can have a directly detrimental effect on the lives of their fellow citizens by virtue of the authority conferred upon them by their role in a state organisation?' As he threw his laptop strap over his shoulder and bent down to pull up the handle of his cabin suitcase and waited for the carriage doors to open, he allowed his train of thought on the semantics of thugs and thuggery to run into the buffers.

He went up the escalator, strolled through the tunnel – he was early and had plenty of time – and walked leisurely to the airport's first barrier where for many years now he had never confronted any hindrance. Once through, however, his armpits began to dampen. It was at the next hurdle, the conveyor belt and security monitors, where he knew that things could go wrong, as they nearly had on a couple of occasions in the recent past. And, if they did, it could well prove costly for him. The art was to take a deep breath, swallow, not to say a word nor allow his feelings to show; he might just manage a smile – though on reflection better not, for that could be construed as a cynical gesture, which could be a punishable offence.

A man wearing surgical rubber gloves placed black plastic crates onto the conveyor rollers. The file of people on the other side, acting like automatons, put their personal belongings into the crates which then passed, like coffins into the crematorium incinerator, through a tunnel where instruments would reveal to a monitoring eye their inner contents. The gloved attendant was in his early forties, of medium height and build. His thinning, fair to gingery hair was parted just off centre and swept back from a slightly freckled forehead making him look distinctly old-fashioned. This image was accentuated by a pair of circular wire-framed glasses – a pre-war design that had recently once again become popular. He was wearing a white, open-necked shirt with rolled-up sleeves revealing the muscular arms of a body builder. In every sense he was everyman; a person forever lost in the crowd, someone who would never, turn a head.

'Take off your belt please, sir. And your shoes,' he said to a stooped octogenarian leaning on a walking stick. 'And, you too, please, madam,' he repeated addressing an equally old lady wearing a tartan tweed suit.

Sebastian squirmed at this demonstration of unbridled authority, civilly expressed but humiliating in effect. Though furious at what he was witnessing he contained his anger and refrained from asking whether the elderly couple had been subjected to such treatment on the grounds that every traveller must be a suspected terrorist. He felt sure that the logic dictating the behaviour of the conveyor belt managers was grounded in an ideology which ran along the lines: 'We have to assume that anyone might be a terrorist. Failure to do so would imply that individuals with certain demographic characteristics are more likely than other people to be selected for screening on the grounds that a risk assessment might deem them to constitute a greater potential threat to the lives of other travellers; such an assumption is discriminatory and a violation of the human rights of individuals with specific profiles.' Therefore, instead of following his inclination and remonstrating against the gratuitous and insulting treatment that he had just witnessed he held his peace and silently looked up and down the man whose demand he regarded as malicious, misanthropic and ill-mannered.

His turn came. Knowing exactly what the procedure required, he was already pulling his arm through his jacket sleeve, when the official virtually snarled the words, 'Take off your jacket.' Sebastian looked him in the eye, hoping that his stare would communicate the contempt he felt for the official confronting him.

'Now your belt.'

'I'm not always required to remove it,' Sebastian bristled.

'I'm asking you to,' the man responded with an implicit threat, in the knowledge that his was the power.

'You're not asking but telling me to, aren't you?' said Sebastian, beginning to unbuckle.

'No, I'm asking you, sir,' said the man, baring his teeth in a sneer reciprocating the antipathy being expressed towards him by the younger male across the conveyor divide.

Sebastian grimaced but did as he had been instructed, then turned away and strolled the few metres to the next hurdle guarded by a shaven-headed man in his mid-thirties wearing a small skull-and-crossbones earring and with the physique of a rugby union loose-head. He heard the voice of the conveyor belt controller call out, but decided to ignore him. Even when the call was repeated a few decibels louder, Sebastian refused to turn around, until the man in front of him, standing akimbo, told him menacingly, 'You're being spoken to, sir.'

Knowing that he was powerless, Sebastian turned

his head. The first guardian of the travellers' safety was holding up a pair of spectacles that Sebastian had placed in the tray in order to pre-empt the possibility of being told to do so.

'We don't want to break these,' he said with a smirk.

'You normally ask for them.' Sebastian tried to regain parity.

'Not this sort. They look too fragile and too easily damaged or even broken.'

Sebastian, looking as hard-faced as he could, took them from the man's hand and turned back towards the final hurdle.

'Stop!' Sebastian heard the now-familiar voice cry out behind his back. Although he had no doubt that the command was directed at him, he chose to disregard it. From an early age he had been constitutionally unable to take orders and had at different stages in his life been punished with varying degrees of severity for his recalcitrance.

'Darren,' the voice called out, 'ask that gentleman to stop, please.' Darren was the shaven-headed, crucifix-wearing St Peter who stood behind, rather than in front of, the pearly portal. His task was to look for any x-ray sign that would allow him to send to purgatory any petitioner seeking permission to pass to the other side. The shout from his colleague, Wayne, signalled to him to withhold consent to the latest applicant for admission to proceed into the beyond.

Sebastian's expression of defiance towards the minor official had been an almost imperceptible movement of his lips. However, despite the fact that he had not emitted any sound at all, he already knew that his petulance would require requital.

'Excuse me, sir. What did you say?' asked the man on the conveyor to Sebastian's back in a loud voice. 'Call the supervisor, please, Darren.' Darren obliged by signalling to a young woman, who nodded her acknowledgement of the request and ambled towards a closed door. She bent and turned the handle, peered inside, raised her leg as a canine to a lamp post and muttered a few words. A man dressed in a black suit appeared, adjusting his tie as he waddled out of his windowless office. He inclined his head towards the woman who explained the incident that she had witnessed. It was definitely a matter that required his attention. Shaking his head and puffing his cheeks he walked towards Sebastian, at the same time hitching up his trousers so that his belt held the waistband at his bulging equator.

'Excuse me, sir, but a member of my staff informs me that you said something abusive to one of her colleagues, who is also a member of my staff.'

'If I did, and I really don't know what I've done or said that could be construed as abusive, then I'm truly very sorry.'

Sebastian began to feel frightened and felt sure that at some point he would be forced to eat humble pie – a slice, yes, but not yet. And the whole pie? No, never. In any case, it was too early to make concessions.

'What exactly am I supposed to have said?' Sebastian asked.

The female interlocutor, who was standing beside her manager, spoke up on behalf of her colleague who, she was sure, had been mortally offended. 'He used the "f" word,' she said, as though the word had never before been pronounced in her company. With bulging eyes and a dropped jaw she said that she would like it to be put on record that it was unimaginable that anyone could say such a thing in polite company, especially not when addressing such a staunch family man as Wayne.

The manager pursed his lips and went over to have a word with Wayne, who was glaring at Sebastian; he asked him a few questions, listened to his answers, and still shaking his head and looking graver than a grave digger, returned to Sebastian. Because of his status as a 'member of management', he had been selected by HR to attend a variety of personal development courses, both day-release and residential, covering issues such as conflict management, the 'psychology of rounding the circle in interpersonal relations', harassment in the workplace, hate speech, discrimination, post-traumatic stress disorder and 'distress'.

Although he hadn't performed so well in the mandatory written tests set by the more expensive training sessions, he always received good grades and commendations for attendance and participation. As a result, he had recently been promoted to the post 'Superior Supervisor, Grade II' – in military terms, the rank of NCO – for his cunning ability to defuse uncomfortable situations which were frequently caused by his Pitbull subordinates; they had been appointed to their posts because they possessed all the necessary physical and psychological characteristics required to make the world a safer place.

'I'm very sorry but I have to request you to… In fact, I'd like to recommend to you in the strongest terms possible that you offer an apology to my member of staff.' He stopped to take breath and gave a sigh; he really wished that he did not have to be put in such embarrassing situations, especially when it required him to act against a person whom he had immediately identified as his social superior. But he had a job to do and this particular task fell within his job description.

'I should tell you though, that Wayne feels so offended by your total lack of respect for him as a person – the actual words he used were "humiliated" and "abused" – that he may not accept an apology. Thankfully, situations like this are very rare, or at least quite rare. On the downside, unfortunately, when they do arise, because this poor man, who is only doing his job, is such an unbelievably kind and sensitive person, he immediately takes any slight to heart. Do you know, a couple of weeks ago he was challenged by a man, much like yourself I have to say, who, because Wayne had asked him to take off his shoes, had the nerve to ask Wayne, "Why are you requiring me to do this? Is it because you think I'm a Muslim terrorist?" You can't imagine how this sort of unthinking question upset him. It was totally out of order.'

The manager paused again and then, shaking his

head, added, 'Some of his colleagues here are Muslim. They share their halal meat sandwiches with him. Do you understand what I'm trying to say? I don't mind confiding in you that after this particular Muslim terrorist episode Wayne had to take a day off work.' He again stopped talking and gave Sebastian what was supposed to be interpreted as a benign, avuncular smile. This was part of a strategy recommended by the teacher on one of the courses he had attended entitled 'Managing the Staff – Public Nexus'. According to the most popular theory currently in circulation, the one being promoted by the course team, good outcomes were achievable when the individual with the authority to punish actually demonstrated compassion, such as smiling.

Another idea central to the strategy that emerged from the theory was the importance of giving the wrong-doer time to reflect on both the injury he or she had caused to a member of staff and on the gravity of the situation in which they had placed themselves.

On the other side of the equation, after having had time to reflect, it was expected that the perpetrator would show remorse by, for example, hanging his head, and then demonstrating repentance through a verbal and truly humble apology.

After a minute's silence, which the Superior Supervisor decided met the requirements of the theory-cum-strategy, he opened his hands, palms up, to Sebastian offering him an opportunity to repent.

'The problem is, I don't know what I'm supposed

to have said that was so insulting,' Sebastian replied. He had been given a chance and was going to take it.

'It was your use of the "f" word which, though not as bad as the "c" word, or the "m" word or above all the "n" word, is nonetheless completely unacceptable, and one which, I'm afraid, we are unable to tolerate and overlook.'

'I'm sorry, but what was this "f" word that I'm supposed to have uttered?' Sebastian was going to continue to bat for the rest of the over and give his best, in the full knowledge that this was a competitive game which he was highly unlikely to ever win.

'As a man of the world, sir, I'm sure that you know what I'm talking about.'

'And if I don't apologise?' Sebastian cocked his head; there were just two more balls to go.

'Then I have no option but to call the police,' the humpty-dumpty manager said, playing his trump card. With one ball to go, Sebastian bowled a googly, or, if you prefer, threw down his joker which was to force the non-commissioned officer to articulate the word.

'Please, before you go to that extreme and call the police, you must tell me what exactly was that word that I am supposed to have used.'

The NCO bent forward slightly and looking Sebastian in the eye spelled out the word f.u.c.k.

Sebastian hesitated for a second, frowned and pulled his head backwards affecting total astonishment at the preposterous and slanderous accusation that these officials were making against him. Then puffing up his chest to give the impression that it was he who had been affronted and should be demanding an apology, he told a brazen lie with total aplomb: 'As a gentleman, I can say in total honesty, that is a word that I never ever use.'

He felt himself to be back on the stage and enacting a role that he had scripted for himself in a play on which the curtain was about to come down.

'Although I've been utterly misinterpreted, I'm going to be quite candid with you, for I have nothing to hide. I did in fact *mouth*, but please take note, I did *not voice* any "f" word. And, the "f" word that I only *mouthed* was emphatically not the one which you have just spelled out; it wasn't the one that your colleagues have libellously attributed to me.' Sebastian licked his dry lips and continued: 'The "f" stands for fascist.'

The black-suited, bulging-bellied Superior Supervisor nodded to the shirt-sleeved conveyor belt controller and, as Sebastian had always feared, he missed his flight.

5

The Contract, the Tenant and the Key

The Contract

Things had been ticking along quite nicely for Geoff, a self-employed consultant hydrologist, and his wife Gloria, a nursery school teacher by training. He had come from a skilled working class background, gained a first class degree from a university which was a member of the Russell Group and whose geology students immediately found work when they graduated. After a few years with a petro-chemical consultancy, which had encouraged him to specialise and to that end financed his studying for a Masters in hydrology and water management, he decided to set up independently.

Ever since his decision to go it alone he had never had to sit twiddling his thumbs waiting for someone to call upon his expertise and neither did he have to search for work; he had established a reputation in his field and during the course of his career had taken on projects for companies of all sizes from multinational corporations to small start-up enterprises.

Because he regularly worked abroad, Gloria, who liked to travel, had chosen to resign from her full-time teaching post and become a supply teacher instead.

They lived a comfortable, childless, Mondeo-man life in exurbia. If asked, they would describe themselves as 'well off but not rich' – unlike one of Geoff's first cousins, Tom, who, owning a large villa in Umbria, was reckoned to fall into that category. He and Geoff were the only two members of their immediate family who others described as 'successful'. However, Geoff and Tom inhabited completely different worlds so that while Geoff and Gloria were aspirational, they did not aspire to the lifestyle that Tom could afford; their ambition was not to become the owners of an estate with electronically controlled gates and a swimming pool in Umbria or Tuscany, but a modest little property anywhere in Italy north of Rome. Gloria had learnt how to manage the envy that she occasionally felt for the financial capacity that Tom's wife, Jessica, had to buy things without thinking twice. She did so by cultivating a sense of personal superiority over her on the sole ground that while she, herself, was qualified and worked, Jessica had always only been a housewife.

Buying a property in Italy was a topic which popped up quite regularly in their conversations, especially after they had watched another television series about Italian architecture, or the regionality of Italian cookery or Italian wine, or the history and role of opera in the Italian way of life. They had accumulated a cabinet of DVD sets of these programmes which, contrary to their stated intention when ordered from Amazon immediately following the programme, they never viewed. Nestled amongst these simulacra were a disorderly pile of CDs, cassettes and DVDs of 'Italian for Beginners'. Two programmes were the exception to this 'bones buried by the dog' behaviour: the first dealt with 'problems and pitfalls associated with buying a house in Italy' and a sequel concentrated on 'buying an older property "full of character" but requiring "extensive restoration"'. These they had watched several times; for some reason it helped them sleep.

One year, as England emerged from the murk of an extraordinarily miserable winter, Geoff received a letter inviting him to an interview at the headquarters of a large firm based in Genoa. He made three phone calls during which he learned from two separate sources that he had been head hunted. The third friend had himself made a couple of calls on Geoff's behalf and discovered that the principal purpose of the meeting was for the company to have a face-to-face conversation with the person who had been recommended to them.

After these two slaps on the back Geoff accepted the invitation. Two days later he caught an early morning flight from City Airport in London, had an intensive three-hour interview, and was taken to a Michelin two-star restaurant for a post-contract-signing lunch before flying back to England in the evening.

The generous fee Geoff was to receive required him to spend three short periods in Italy over the next two years, beginning that September. This meant that he and Gloria could start to turn the dream about owning a property in Italy into reality.

It was mid-June, just before the holiday season took off, when the couple set out on a two-week exploratory visit. They crossed the French border at Modane, travelled through the Frejus tunnel then took the road through Susa towards Turin, which they skirted, and turned south to Cuneo, emerging on the coast at Ventimiglia, just twenty-odd miles east of Monaco. Their search started as soon as they arrived in Imperia. After browsing the windows of local estate agents it quickly became clear that the price which they would have to pay would be a good deal higher than the income Geoff would receive from his new contract.

By the end of the first week, they had visited half a dozen small, dilapidated farmhouses, perched isolated, high up on densely forested hillsides, four of them at the end of goat tracks and a twenty-minute drive to the nearest hamlet. Such properties, quaintly described by estate agents as *un rustico*, were categorically crossed off their list of buildings to be viewed. Apart from their desolate locations, not only was life too short to be put at the mercy of builders with their ingrained habit of devouring time like a cormorant, but there was the cost; even if a building with a red-tiled roof and a paneless skylight to the night was *not* the temporary home of a shepherd and possibly his sheep and *not* in need of total reconstruction, it invariably required the installation of electricity and running water and a more efficient twentieth-century septic tank.

Not one of the properties they had been shown within their price range could they ever envisage calling 'home'. Nonetheless, despite their disappointing start, they had convinced themselves that they should stop regarding the holiday as merely an 'exploratory visit'. Instead of saying that they 'hoped' to find a house, they would henceforth be more positive and speak of being 'more than sure' that by the end of the two weeks they would have found a little bit of *terra firma* in the Mediterranean that they could call their own. Such was their optimism that they joked about how their main challenge was no longer about *finding* a property but how to 'make the one correct choice' from amongst all the properties they had seen and were yet to view. By this time next year, they mused, the two of them would be relaxing, and eating and drinking in a setting that until recently had been the prerogative of the wealthy, the literati and artists from all over northern Europe.

A week had passed and they were half way through their holiday when they were shown a small, pink house covered in a flourishing bougainvillea. It sat on a promontory with a panoramic view across the bay to Portofino and within a short walking distance of a clustering of shops in a tiny fishing hamlet huddled in a cove underneath a railway viaduct – a characteristic feature of long stretches of the Ligurian coastline. The property also had its own private bathing area reached by sixty-five steeply descending steps, some of which were the interstices between the roots of maritime pines whose trunks leant out in a right-angle salute to the sea. The descent was so steep that, decades earlier, the very well-off Milanese owners of the main villa had installed a small cable car to carry its passengers up and down. Now the rusted cabin sat amongst the trees as a memento of an early twentieth-century whimsy or perhaps of the owner's fascination with Italian Futurism's delight in mechanical technology.

The bougainvillea-clad bijou being offered to Geoff and Gloria formed part of the patrimony of the original owners' daughter, who was selling it to finance not the culturally rich way of life to which she and her surgeon husband were accustomed, but the sybaritic lifestyle of their adult offspring who were yet to find gainful and permanent employment. As members of the *haute bourgeoisie* they were being forced to adjust to changing circumstances as had Don Fabrizio, the Prince of Salina, in his endeavour to preserve the family's residual feudal power in Sicily during Italy's struggle for unification. They too, in the twilight of the twentieth century, were prisoners of history, of their culture and the customs of their class and society; and they were just as eager as *il principe* to maintain their material privileges and exclusive status. Disposing of the small house that had until a year ago been the home of a three-generation Neapolitan family, who had serviced them and her parents in all sorts of ways over many years, would offer the Milanese family a respite.

However, the private concerns of the owners and the way in which the issues that preoccupied them were intertwined with their ruminations on Italy's tumultuous history were far from the minds of Geoff and Gloria; their foremost worry was that the spectacular views from the cottage patio and its personal status-enhancing situation came at a price. The estate agent had warily avoided this disagreeable topic until he had shown them the property and allowed them time to imbibe the totality of its 'incomparable' setting. When that moment came, a quick piece of mental arithmetic told them that, if they were to buy it, then whether in Italy or in England, eating anything much more than a daily helping of pasta and a green salad, with a meat dish once a week and fish on Friday would, for some time to come, be classified as luxury living.

However it was not just a cottage and tiny patio that they were buying. The price included a diminuitve bathing area – in fact, a slab of rock – at the bottom of the steps, a metre or so above the deep, lapping water. This private space was just out of hearing distance of the vendor's far larger basking patch to which a small boat was tethered. While drawing special attention to the two most precious attributes of the bathing sites – their almost total privacy and spectacular unbroken view across the bay – the imperious matriarch, the lawyer in the family, made it clear with an open-mouthed smile bursting with insincerity that the occupants of the villa did not expect Geoff and Gloria to stray off their concrete handkerchief.

After the tour and the exchange of monosyllabic pleasantries over a light seafood lunch, mediated by the estate agent, Geoff said through their interpreter that they would give serious thought to the wonderful opportunity being presented to them.

As the English couple drove away they began to find reasons why this house, despite its wonderful location, was not for them.

'It's not the money,' Geoff said. 'Or, not just a matter of money, although that comes into it. The point is that I didn't think it was us. Do you know what I mean?'

'Oh, I agree, totally,' Gloria said, turning to look at him. Then, resting back in her bucket seat and checking her lipstick in the mirror behind the pulled-down sunshield, she gave a subdued sigh and added with an under-the-breath reluctance, 'We wouldn't fit in, would we?' Both she and Geoff had their individual sense of status and of where they stood in social hierarchies. They had their doubts about the house itself, but it was the vendors who had in most unsubtle ways left them feeling uncomfortable.

'I don't think that their standoffishness had anything to do with us,' Gloria continued self-comfortingly. 'They didn't really want anyone to live there, apart from servants. Which, I suppose, is fair enough, given their backgrounds.' As far as Gloria was concerned, their social class, which was an amalgam of 'family', upbringing, education and 'old money', was a legitimate reason for their aloofness. She also guessed that their unfriendly snootiness had something to do with the resentment they felt at having to dismiss the caretaker and his dependants in order to cover some of the expenses of their two clearly overindulged and indolent progeny. On top of that Gloria surmised that the Milanese looked down their noses at any foreigner whose aspiration to buy a property in such an elite location was limited to living in the former servants' quarters. Not wanting to admit being rankled, they turned from the owners to the house itself.

'From the moment that our Omar Sharif lookalike estate agent pointed it out to us when we were in his smart Mercedes sports, I thought to myself that the whole scene seemed a bit pretentious,' Geoff said turning his head from the road ahead to look at Gloria.

'Oh, you're just jealous of his good looks. That's why you're calling it pretentious,' Gloria joked. 'Forget about him. The problem is that the house opens directly onto the main coast road from Rapallo to Sestri Levante. There's no way that anyone living in that house could insulate themselves against the noise of the traffic that throttles along it.'

Geoff laughed: 'You're dead right! Can you imagine all those scooters and motorbikes racing past the house at all hours of the day and night?'

★

As they drove to the next town on their planned itinerary, they re-examined the criteria guiding their search. The rustic farmhouse had already been crossed off their list; they agreed that this type of property should be left to much younger people; not only did they have longer time horizons and greater energy, but they would find physical labour and the sacrifice of comfort novel experiences. At the other end of the continuum apartments in condominiums furnished with heavy, dark-stained, fitted wardrobes made of laminated wood were also ruled out. Though noise was firmly on the proscribed list, they shook their heads and laughed at the thought of ever being able to insist on peace and quiet as a necessary condition for their choice.

At the beginning of their third week, they came off the arterial highway that runs along the coast between Livorno and the Franco-Italian border, and drove into a largish town on the boundary between Tuscany and Liguria, whose former strategic significance is marked by a fortress on a hill above it and a citadel originally built by the Pisans. They had phoned ahead and were on time for their appointment at an estate agency managed by a bright and cheerful young woman, Isella. To judge from her knowledge of English, which she had studied at university, she had been a good student. She took them on a two-day tour of a dozen properties, reserving the best to last, knowing that this would be the easiest to sell. It was a detached house with stupendous views across the narrow coastal plain to the Apuan Mountains.

The price exceeded by a small margin the maximum that they had set for themselves – which was almost double the amount they had calculated that they could afford, taking into account Geoff's windfall. At that precise moment in time, however, the financial aspect of their decision to buy the house was ranked as 'of lesser importance'.

The owner accepted their agent-brokered offer. They all shook hands and Geoff proposed a small toast to Isella's much appreciated diligence. Antonio Bettini, the owner, praised her ability to get things done without fuss and with such charm. She thanked them for being such good-humoured and easy-going clients and agreed to arrange and complete the necessary formalities, including a meeting at the notary's office for the signing of the contract.

Geoff and Gloria, overjoyed at their good fortune, decided to celebrate by eating in a nearby candlelit and expensive restaurant rather than at the cheap motel in which they were staying, whose accommodation one of them described as similar to a 'cheerless remand cell'.

Two days later, just as they were finishing their meagre breakfast of tasteless bread rolls and weak coffee, the manager brought them a message saying that Isella would like to meet them at ten o'clock that morning in the Café del Teatro near her office. She had also stressed that she needed to see them urgently because she had received some bad news.

Geoff and Gloria were, as usual, on time. Isella,

unusually, was already sitting at a table with a glass of water. She stood up as they came in, ordered coffee for Geoff, English breakfast tea for Gloria and a green tea for herself.

In a nutshell, the day after their meeting with the vendor she had received a call from a hitherto unmentioned Swiss citizen who had, Isella now informed them, already declared an interest in the house. Isella had not mentioned her to them before because she thought that this other potential client had faded away. However, she felt quite sure that the Swiss woman could be persuaded to buy another, more expensive, property that had just come onto the market and perfectly suited her requirements.

'Doesn't sound too good,' Geoff said stoically.

Geoff had had his doubts about this competitor as soon as she had been introduced into their purchasing equation. As Isella's account unfolded he became less and less convinced about its authenticity. As a result he discounted this 'piece of bad news' as constituting a real problem and waited to hear what other bad news she was going to present to them. This she delivered in a head-bent-forward, conspiratorial whisper.

'The gossipy word that has filtered through to me, which I'm now going to decant into your ears – not a bad expression, don't you think? – is that the Italian legal owner of the house, Antonio Bettini, and his female Dutch cohabitee are separating.' She let the information have time to be interpreted and then continued: 'To make matters worse, the house which this faltering-in-love couple want to buy has been taken off the market.' Again wanting the seriousness of her stark and clearly stated message to sink in, she folded her arms on the table and looked Gloria firmly in the eye knowing that it was the woman whom she needed to impress most with her bad tidings before turning her gaze to Geoff.

'Whatever the truth of the gossip, which incidentally I heard from my dentist, who happens to be the brother of the owner's girlfriend, there's a strong chance that he or they will change their minds about going ahead with the sale whether to you or anyone else.' Isella paused again before concluding: 'I'm ever so sorry to be the bringer of so much bad news, but I thought that I should tell you right away.'

'You were absolutely correct to do so, Isella,' Geoff said calmly. 'Nevertheless, I assume that the deal's going through unless you tell us otherwise.' Geoff's personality fitted his chosen profession and his profession benefited from his character.

'Exactly,' Isella confirmed, not sure whether Geoff could make that assumption nor what she could do to avert unpleasantness should any of the obstacles that she had mentioned prevent the transaction from being completed.

What Isella did not know was that as far as her two English clients were concerned they had agreed to purchase *that* house and would not be prevented from doing so by the appearance of anyone else with an interest in buying it, marital discord or Italian prevarication. Though she had her weaknesses, nobody who knew Gloria would disagree that one of her outstanding strengths was an astonishing tenacity. This virtue, of which she was proud, combined with an ability to adroitly negotiate and compromise was well rewarded; a week later the transaction was completed in the office of the notary, the stout and cravatted Signor Capelli.

The buyers handed over a cheque, recorded by the notary, who duly witnessed the signing and transfer of the property deeds. This part of the purchasing procedure registered *'for fiscal purposes'* the official, albeit grossly undervalued, price that had been paid for the house. The Genovese vendor, together with Geoff and Gloria, then went into the notary's antechamber, where they handed over a substantial amount of money in cash, which represented the difference between the informally agreed and formally registered price.

Although everyone involved in the transaction was happy with the outcome, Geoff and Gloria now had to decide how they were going to fund their venture. A manageable, short-term bridging loan would have to be found to cover the difference between the actual price of the house and their savings plus the value of Geoff's contract. Besides the capital cost of the purchase they also needed money to pay for the running and maintenance of their acquisition. A few jottings on a serviette established above all reasonable doubt what they had long suspected: since their joint incomes from all sources would be insufficient to cover the costs of two households and a new lifestyle, to which they had in their minds already become accustomed, their new acquisition would have to be rented out for part of the year. This would mean entering into another contract.

The Tenant

Sitting on the terrace beneath an orange tree, sipping their *aperitivi* while drinking in the landscape of their freshly acquired home, they chortled at their good luck and Geoff congratulated Gloria for her bulldog behaviour which had enabled them, against considerable odds, to buy a house with a view to match that of the pink gem overlooking Portofino.

The land in front of the house was given over to vines and a scattering of fruit trees which cascaded down in a series of terraces to a stream out of their view. Swivelling their eyes to their left, they could see, across a dip gouged out of the limestone terrain, the turret of a ruined medieval castle which towered over a knot of ancient, mainly light grey, multi-storeyed houses with red-tiled roofs that formed the town's defensive wall. These in turn sat broodingly above a higgledy-piggledy ensemble of newer houses painted in various shades of yellow. When they raised their eyes above the vineyard to look directly ahead they could see, as if to touch, the Apuan Alps and the marble mountains of Carrara, where Michelangelo had come to select a block of marble from which, when shipped to Florence, he would sculpt his *David*.

'Inspirational' was the word that came to mind when they wanted to describe the awesome grandeur of the panorama from their patio. It was not until long after the sun had set, the moon had ascended over the trees and the temperature fallen a couple of degrees so that Geoff had to roll down his shirt sleeves, that they went back into the house. Over supper their conversation turned once again from musing about their good luck and the beauty that lay all around them to focusing more practically on the depressing question of how they would find the money to pay the piper who had lured them to their eagle's perch.

A few days later their spirits were unexpectedly raised by their estate agent, whom they had arranged to meet in order to plunder her address book and stored knowledge for information on a whole range of issues that a person new to an area needed to know, such as the names, addresses and reputation of local tradesmen. Isella answered all the questions on their list, phoned the three utility companies and arranged to accompany her English clients to their offices and set up accounts.

When all these basic formalities covering normal day-to-day basic needs for water, electricity and gas had been completed and they were returning to the car park, Isella mentioned that she had a partner in England, Jocasta Leonelli, an Englishwoman who was married to an Italian.

★

They had barely set foot back inside their house in the East Midlands before Gloria was on the phone to Mrs Leonelli to follow up the link Isella had given to her. Of course, Jocasta knew Isella, whom she referred to as 'a terrific young woman, full of sparkle and very good with clients'. For Gloria, all those particles of sparkling dust of good luck that had been so generously sprinkled over their shoulders continued to glitter.

'Oh, you're not the first couple to fall in love with Italy and then find a house that you can't really afford,' Mrs Leonelli said reassuringly. 'You're also not the first to want to find people to rent your property to help defray the costs of running it.'

'I thought that might be the case,' Gloria said with a sigh of relief. The fact that there were other people in the same boat, perhaps a titanic number of them all trying to avoid drowning in debt, meant that agencies and channels must exist to supply lifebelts of one sort or another.

'I've seen pictures of your place and I'm absolutely certain that you'll have no problems in letting it. In fact, I know someone who, I'm pretty sure, will be delighted to rent it. He's just taken early retirement and comes along to an Italian evening class in our village that's run by a friend of mine. Whenever I see him he tells me how he wishes he could find a place to stay in Italy where he could enjoy practising his language skills.'

'Really?' Gloria looked up to heaven and shook her head at both this piece of welcome news and at the water stain below the moulded plaster cornice which Geoff had promised to deal with.

'Has he been studying long?'

'Oh, my God, yes. Yonks. He just loves the language. We've often joked that he should go there to live. And when we say that he always replies that perhaps he will one day. Anyway, the crucial point for you is that he's the sort of person who'll just fit in with your needs and arrange to go out there whenever your house in Liguria is available. He's called Henry but known to everyone as Harry.'

'But, surely, this Harry must have been to Italy before,' Gloria said quizzically. 'As you say Italy doesn't suffer from a shortage of holiday lets.'

'Oh, absolutely. There's a huge market and Harry's rented on several occasions, but they seem to be either enormous villas, sleeping eight or more people, or rather dingy flats. The place that you've just bought, take it from me, would suit him down to the ground.'

They chatted on for a while, agreed to keep in contact and finished with Jocasta giving her Harry's phone number. By the end of the day, Gloria had rung him, had a brief conversation and come to a most agreeable, almost perfect, arrangement.

★

A routine emerged with little effort on either side: just when Europe was turning its back on winter, Harry would telephone and ask if the house was vacant at a particular time, usually in May, adding that he would probably like to go out for another week or two again in September or early October, on condition that those dates were convenient for them, emphasising that he was totally flexible around his proposed dates. As with the few other clients who had responded to their advertisement in an inexpensive and rather old-fashioned magazine, Geoff and Gloria never met Harry. All contact was by telephone with confirmation by letter and accompanying cheque. He was the goose who twice a year laid his egg without fuss.

From the little information that Harry gave them about his travel plans and stay they gathered that he either flew to Pisa where he rented a car to make the forty-minute journey to the house, or he drove from England with one other person, often a relative. Having pitched camp, he would normally be joined by a couple of visitors, who would come out for long weekends or short mid-week breaks, depending on the availability of cheap airfares.

Besides providing his guests with accommodation, Harry would show them around the local villages, and be their guide along well-maintained footpaths through the woodlands and across spectacular cliff tops. Visitors adored the bumpy drive down a track to a rather rundown farmstead, where a toothless and wizened old woman would come out of the house at the sound of a car's engine and go to the barn, where the wine was kept in state-approved and monitored stainless-steel vats, and refill their three-litre flagons. They were equally appreciative of the longer drive to one particular estate north of Lucca where they bought estate-bottled wines and farm-produced olive oil, dried mushrooms and tomatoes to take home to England as presents.

At the end of their short stay, it was quite normal for guests to repay Harry's hospitality by inviting him out to supper. While most would take him to a 'good-value-for-money' trattoria that he had himself recommended, occasionally one of his better-off friends would treat him to lunch or dinner in a more expensive restaurant.

Over the years Harry had proved himself time and again to be the ideal tenant. An actuary by profession who had spent most of his working life with one large insurance company, he was by nature highly practical. Given his cast of mind, when something in the house in Italy malfunctioned, not only did he *not* complain, it came as second nature to repair or replace it and not tell the owners that he had done so. In truth, he belonged to that category of people who actually enjoy tackling minor jobs, whether unblocking the sink or rehanging the door. Another reason for fixing things in and around the house was that he saw no sense in living in discomfort when he knew how simple it would be to mend or put right whatever it might be without too much effort.

Similarly, if he was sitting on the terrace, reading, and from the corner of his eye noticed that a plant was wilting for lack of water, he would put down the book, walk around to the back of the house, fill the watering can, return and pour the nourishing liquid over the withering green leaves. He knew that the task could have waited, but he also knew that it would be futile to tell himself to ignore the distraction, relax and do it later. To do so would be contrary to a principle according to which he lived his life: whatever blemished his immediate, visible surroundings had to be dealt with there and then. That was the man: someone for whom, until now, the wild and unkempt orchard at Grantchester would have caused more distress than pleasure.

The whole environment, from the internal layout of the house on via Cavour, its furnishing, especially the kitchen, and the flowers and the orange, lemon and almond trees on the terraces around it, to the weekly market in the piazza and the cultural events in the castle, could not be more different to the bungalow and Surrey countryside, where he had lived from the beginning of his working life. Of course, age played its part in his maturing view of the world; with the passage of time he had been liberated from the burden of a mortgage and suddenly become less concerned about insurance, whether on the house, the car or his life.

One day, while out walking, he suddenly paused, rolled his lower lip against his teeth, screwed up his eyes to stare across the sea-encroaching plain to the mountains and nodded his head. *Yes*, he thought, *I'm as much at home here as in Surrey* – except for one thing: although he had good reading skills, his spoken Italian – which had been the much-talked-about reason for his renting the house in the first place – had not improved as much as he had anticipated. On the other hand, despite his lack of command of the vernacular, he had mastered the art of sustaining fairly lengthy conversations with his immediate neighbours and engaging with the bar owners and older residents whom he met in the street, small grocery store and in the bar – not so much by talking himself but by listening and paying attention to the way individuals communicated through body language.

Gradually, Harry came to gain a better understanding of what seemed to be clandestine, mostly unspoken but ever present, enmities that were more than suspicious jealousies found in small rural communities. Different conversational conduits converged on one primary cause for these ill-feelings: events that occurred towards the end of the Second World War – in August 1944 the German army established the Gothic Line, its final defensive line in northern Italy. This encompassed the village and house which Harry currently occupied.

Not far from one of the more imposing villas in the village, which had been sequestered for the use of a German regional commander, and snuggling into a recess on a sharp bend in the road leading out of the village, was a crudely cut memorial stone. The plaque above it commemorated two Italians who had been shot less than a month before the end of the war. Only the names of the two men together with their dates of birth and execution were given.

The ambivalent accounts that Harry received to his innocent questions about the men – who they were and why they had been shot (murdered?) – revealed the broken seams and frayed edges in the community's social fabric that had been caused or exacerbated by events that occurred half a century ago.

Although it was more likely that they had been partisans rather than collaborators or black marketeers, the frugality of the description of the event given to him by different individuals provided fertile ground for speculation. Listening to the different, always vague, explanations brought home to Harry that his lack of fluency in the language prevented him from gaining any real insight into why, outwardly, life in the village was bursting with jollity and vitality, while, internally, the inhabitants wrestled with a buried melancholy.

As the years passed, Harry contrived to be alone in Italy for ten continuous days at a time, allowing him to venture into the less touristic, dark, Grimm fairy tale mountains of the Garfagnana. On one of his excursions he drove up the Lima river valley to Bagni di Lucca, once famous for its thermal baths and for being the home to the 'first casino in Europe', where Liszt and Puccini performed and the Romantic poets Shelley, Byron and Heine had spent time. The appeal of the place lay not only in its association with that past, but also because of its shabbiness and decay, despite the recent restoration of the casino building as a museum, and the refurbishment of a few of its nineteenth-century thermal baths. The place was, as it had been in its heyday, a Romantic's rejection of order, harmony and tranquillity and rationality.

On another visit to this area he drove through the spa along a winding road that went deep into the mountains and came to a dead end in the village of Montefegatesi. He parked his car and walked up through the lanes of this depopulated settlement to a high vantage point. For an hour or more he sat there on a wooden, slatted bench that had been set down on a tiny, more-dust-than-gravel patch of land surrounded by a few shrivelled plants and next to a monument to Dante. He never forgot his first impression:

The breath-taking view from this position reminded him of the painting of *The Wanderer above a Sea of Fog* by Caspar David Friedrich. Although Harry had been dressed in shorts and not a nineteenth-century frock coat, he identified with the picture of the Wanderer that hung in his mind's hall of memorable images. The picture acclaimed the solitariness of the individual who at that moment gained an insight into life's precariousness and simultaneously its absurdity and futility.

The subject of the painting is a tousle-haired man standing with his back to the viewer on a perlious outcrop. He is resting casually on his walking stick, and gazing towards a series of mountain pinnacles protruding through a mist which shrouds the mysterious and unknowable world. His whole dress and posture is that of a man who, having just left his comfortable, tastefully furnished home in the frenetic city to go out for a stroll, suddenly finds himself alone in this barren, uninhabited landscape. Harry imagined that this man had turned his back on society and was facing the challenge presented by raw, untamed nature. Sitting there in the fading autumn sunshine Harry raised his eyebrows at the lightbulb realisation that this painting, which he had seen in the Kunsthalle in Hamburg thirty years ago, had been lying dormant in his memory quietly nurturing his will to embark on a voyage to discover another state of being.

Now, as he gazed down from the Dante memorial to the soft haze lying like a duvet over the sharp, serrated mountains folding down to the sea, thirty-odd miles to the south and invisible from where he stood, he was that wanderer, revelling in a deepening appreciation of nature and overwhelmed by the feeling of the sublime. Harry, who had regarded himself as the most ordinary of men, began to gain a sense of his extraordinary self and to feel the elation of being the master of all that he surveyed. Returning to the car he looked back on all those other occasions walking in the hills or sitting on the terrace, when he had consciously reflected on the bliss of his self-imposed monastic silence. The euphoria caused by his epiphany only began to fade and his thoughts veer to more prosaic matters when he reached the coast and turned onto a side road that climbed up to his home.

One evening, after an *al fresco* supper, soaking in the silence, these disparate symbols – Dante's monument, the Caspar David Friedrich painting, the war time commemorative plaque – came together and Harry resolved to commit himself to another way of living.

The Key

For more than ten years after buying the house, Geoff and Gloria had been content to draw a modest income from renting it out in order to pay off their small loan and offset the cost of its running and maintenance. Over time the number of weeks when they made the house available for letting was gradually reduced until, one day, they decided that the rent paid by their one regular tenant, Harry, was sufficient to pay utility bills and local taxes. With the removal of the need to draw an income from renting, Geoff and Gloria began to drive or fly to Italy more often, together as a couple or individually with a friend, much as Harry did.

Eventually, with the maturation of a few bonds and other small investments, they felt that they could afford to cease being *rentiers*; it was a status which always sat awkwardly with their work ethic and inherited attitude towards unearned income. Harry now came to present them with a moral dilemma: he had been an exemplary and loyal tenant for as long as they had owned the house and yet now they wanted to tell him that from next Easter the house was to be used solely by them and members of their extended family.

After toying with a number of alternative ways of informing him about their decision, they concluded that the best way of not hurting his feelings would be to meet up with him for lunch at a celebrity chef restaurant somewhere in Surrey, when they would express their gratitude for his having been such a good tenant and then tell him that they intended to sell the house. Incredibly, this would be the first and last time that the three of them ever met. Unable to make up their minds on the most appropriate way to communicate their news and terminate their long-standing relationship, they plumped for delaying their decision on 'the how and where' to tell him until the autumn.

Friends of Gloria and Geoff had gone out for Easter and Harry had followed them, and, as if preternaturally warned, he had asked whether they minded if he stayed on longer than usual. Naturally, in view of their embarrassment caused by genuine feelings of guilt about their plan to deny him further use of the house, they replied immediately by telling him that, 'You can stay as long as you like.' They were sure that the fact that they were not setting a time limit did not mean that he would interpret their invitation literally; they calculated that on the basis of his behaviour over many years, he only had in mind to extend his stay by a week, or at the outside, two weeks. Their letter intimated that there was no rush for him to leave nor any need for him to reply with specific dates.

With the school holidays still over a month away and Harry due to leave, Gloria and Geoff set off on a leisurely drive down through the Alsace, crossing the Rhine at Strasbourg and down to Basle, around Lake Lucerne and through the Gotthard Pass. When they left the A1 *autostrade* to join the A15 towards Parma and La Spezia they noticed purply black storm clouds swirling over the Apuans as if gathering for a black mass. Two vivid and dramatic forked lightning flashes were followed by a shuddering overhead thunderclap which boomed the arrival of the rain.

First, a few heavy raindrops pattered on the bonnet and the windscreen. These were the prelude to the deluge. The wipers working at top speed could not clear the screen of water. Geoff, gripping the steering wheel, his head bent forward, could hardly see the two lanes ahead and Gloria had covered her eyes with her hands. A huge truck appeared in front of them and another eighteen-metre-long drawbar lorry signalled and rumbled past. This was not the first time that they had been terrified when they had found themselves driving into a Mediterranean thunderstorm, but none was as frightening as the present one. Fortunately, the sky blast was short-lived; the first shot of blue was a signal for the sun to peep out and then begin a game of hide and seek with the clouds before finally emerging triumphant in the sky. The storm was over and to celebrate their survival, they stopped for a coffee at the next service station.

By late afternoon they were parking their car in a marked space across the road from their house. Geoff grabbed the larger suitcase from the boot and rushed ahead. He angled his way through their gate, went down a set of wide, broken steps, and panted along their narrow terrace to the front door of the house where, giving a huge puff, he dropped the case.

Next to the door was a large fuchsia-filled terracotta pot which he tilted to reach under for the key, since this is where Harry always put it when he had locked up and was prepared to leave. He was still groping around when Gloria arrived.

'Here you are, take my key,' she said, handing it to him. He inserted it into the lock; it seemed a bit stiff, but that was not unusual. Then he realised that he had inserted it in the wrong way around, which was easily done.

'Oh, give it to me,' said Gloria primly. But after reinserting it correctly, the key still wouldn't turn. 'I'll get the other set from the car,' Geoff replied gruffly in retaliation to Gloria's fussiness. He returned with a larger bunch of keys which included one to their metal letter box attached to the porch wall.

Imagining that had there been a torrential thunderstorm, like the one that they had encountered a couple of hours earlier, just when Harry was about to depart, Geoff guessed that he would probably have posted the keys in the letter box rather than fumble around trying to put them under the pot. Following his intuition, Geoff selected the small key to the green postbox and opened it.

Inside were the routine circulars and leaflets with supermarket special offers together with electricity, water and telephone bills – all paid by standing order – and a tax demand from the local council. Amongst this dull collection were two letters with their names handwritten on the envelopes. While one did not have the address of the sender, on the reverse of the other was the office stamp of the Italian estate agent through whom they had originally bought the house. Geoff handed the latter to Gloria and opened the other, which contained a short note from Harry, which he read out.

Dear Geoff and Gloria,

I would like to thank you both from the bottom of my heart for giving me the opportunity to buy no.7 via Cavour. It was extremely kind of your nephew to let me know that it was coming on to the market. I can honestly say that I've enjoyed every moment spent here – in fact, so much so that as the years have stolen past us, I've come to regard the house more and more as 'home'. The first two weeks of my holiday were blissful and I shall be eternally grateful to you for allowing me to extend my stay for a further two since it was then that I realised that the very walls were crying out for me to stay; every item in the house seemed to be declaring that it belonged to me. The emotional bond that has come to exist between me, the house and its surroundings means that I have no alternative but to move in and live here permanently, which I intend to do at the end of the summer. If I'm here all year long, I know that within a short time I'll be sufficiently fluent in Italian to be able to blend much more fully into the community.

Because with the passage of time you and I have established such a good relationship, should you ever want to come back and stay in the house to enjoy its views and everything it has to offer, I'll be only too pleased to rent it out to you – but, I have to say, only on an occasional basis. Since you must be at the house now, should you want to stay rather than rent somewhere else, just contact the estate agent, who has been so marvellously helpful and has the key.

Affectionately yours,

Harry

Gloria had hesitated before opening the letter from the estate agent. But as soon as Geoff had finished reading Harry's she tore open the other envelope with a trembling hand and handing it to Geoff said with a tear in her eye, 'You read it to me.'

Dear Geoff and Gloria,

As you know, I always had my doubts about your idea of transferring the ownership of your house to your less well-off niece and nephew, in order to avoid complications with inheritance tax in the future. However, as it is my policy never to meddle in my clients' affairs, when I was approached to sell the house on via Cavour I followed all the correct procedures. I consulted the original notary, Signor Capelli – whom you might remember and who sends you his regards – to verify the signature etc. Having been assured that everything was correct from a legal point of view, I felt satisfied that I could proceed to fulfil the instructions given to me by your niece and nephew to dispose of the property.

You will be pleased to know that it was snapped up immediately by another English gentleman who has been on our books for many years, waiting as he put it 'for the right property to come along'. I should add that both the vendor and purchaser paid our agency a generous commission.

My parents have asked me to tell you that you should be very proud of your young relatives, who like you have behaved impeccably. I'm sure that your family's decision is in everyone's best interest. This letter is being sent to the present address at the express wishes of the vendor.

Yours sincerely,

Isella (on behalf of Casedelsoli)

6

From Mackeson to Mâcon

'Dad would like to go out to have a small beer with you, when you go,' she said to him after his late light supper of bacon and eggs. Although she had never said this before, he imagined that it was not the first time that she had formulated this or a similar suggestion in her head to put to him during one of his regular, though fleeting and infrequent, visits. He could never be sure whether, whenever his mother said such a thing about him and his father 'doing something together', it was out of a genuine concern for her husband or whether she was voicing her irritation with him for some petty failing on his part.

Unwilling to speak out on her own behalf and express what she wanted for herself, she transferred on to her son her brooding mood of mild aggression towards his father, which on the face of it had its origin in the fact that he was a highly sociable extrovert while she was more introverted and embarrassingly shy – a trait which she tried to disguise in company by smiling and laughing loudly. In contrast to these emotions that lay within conscious reach, her feelings of extreme disappointment about his conspicuousness as an outsider were so deeply buried that they were beyond detection. It was the latter that probably constituted the source of her aggression and, since it was so inaccessible, was untreatable. One event, which stuck in Tony's memory, supported his belief of what motivated his mother's behaviour.

He had been in his early twenties and living in London. His rented flat at the top of a five-storey, red-brick Edwardian house on the Finchley Road, beneath which the Metropolitan line rumbled well into the night, was not exactly squalid; that term was reserved to describe the bathroom and lavatory, one floor down, which he and his flatmate shared with other short-term-let tenants.

This was the insalubrious habitat in which he lodged his parents during their weekend visit to see him and meet his current partner with whom he seemed to be seriously involved. He had arranged a weekend of events for them: a West End show on the Saturday and supper at the home of a friend's parents on the Sunday. Everything had gone well, but on the last night, he had left them rather abruptly to go and sleep with his girlfriend. The next morning he had seen them off at Waterloo. A few days later he received a letter from his mother. It was brief, as her letters always were, and began with the words, 'I'm not one for words or writing, even though

I do like doing the crossword in the *Evening Gazette*. But because of the way you treated us I feel I must say something.'

The words that most stood out from the page then and rang in his ears now were 'hurt' and 'disrespectful'. However, she made it quite clear that she was not the person 'hurt' or who found his action that night 'disrespectful' – 'It's your father who has taken it very badly.' Much later, reflecting on the occasion, he concluded that, although his father would not have chosen those exact words, they could have matched his sentiments, which he might just have expressed to her. Tony's conduct almost certainly would have upset and offended him, largely because he would have expected his well-educated son to have behaved in an altogether more gentlemanly fashion. But the words? Tony had from the beginning strongly suspected that it was his respectable working class mother who had been affronted, and it was she who felt, as she would have said, 'slighted'.

He recalled how that letter had brought home to him what he really knew but chose to push aside: that he had behaved badly and deserved to be rebuked. His immediate reaction at the time had been to take the next day off work and catch the early morning train to visit his parents. Following this act of homage he returned to London on the midnight Royal Mail sorting train.

What she had now just said about 'going for a beer' fell into the same category; it was a rebuke posing as a reminder addressed by a parent to an adult child to be

respectful. The word that she never used was 'debt'.
Neither, he thought, should she, since children can have
no debt to their parents for it is in nature's unwritten
compact that the latter should give what they can to their
offspring, who, in the fullness of time, will return that gift
by passing on what they can to their own children. The
fact that the way in which this is done is often bungled
does not affect the indelibility of the intergenerational
covenant. The mistakes that usually occur during the
lengthy process of its gifting can be distressing, yet
at the same time, are blissful manifestations of our
metaphorical fall from grace and encapsulated in the
saying *errare humanum est*.

He always let them know beforehand when he would be
coming down and on which train. The train he travelled on
invariably arrived mid-evening after they had finished their
supper and he either walked or took a taxi from the station.
He knew that they would calculate how long this last stage
in his journey would take and therefore know when to
listen out for a car stopping with its engine running or for
a ring at the door. One of them would pull the curtain on
the first floor bay window of their rented flat just to check;
his father would then go down to let him in and his mother
would go into the tiny kitchen to fry his bacon and eggs,
which he ate alone while they returned to the sitting room
and the television, where he joined them after he had eaten.

This was the beginning of one of life's rituals in

which filial duty pairs with parental prerogative. The clean and tidy chapel in which he joined them had been wallpapered by his father, most recently in a striped design which, though not overly elaborate, he had failed to properly align. A large faded poster of Constable's *The Hay Wain* in a cheap gilded frame purchased from a local charity shop hung over the prettily tiled Edwardian fireplace, currently occupied by a three-bar electric fire. The room's only source of heating was enlivened by strips of scarlet red plastic shaped into a child's hand-held windmill; these rotated underneath a translucent moulded cover that had been crudely painted to represent a heap of glowing coal.

A rarely used, shining new, veneered chipboard dining table and four plastic-seated chairs, purchased as part of a dining room suite at the Co-op with the help of her dividend points, sat in the bay. One wall was taken up by a sideboard stuffed with bedding and towels and whose two drawers contained every piece of documentary evidence that proved their existence: life and funeral insurance policies of a lamentably low value, the rent book, a Co-op coupon stamp book, an untidy bunch of letters – nearly all from Tony and his father's sister, whom he hadn't seen since before *the* war – a handful of seaside holiday postcards, and a few Brownie camera photos – mostly loose but with a few hinged into two miniature albums.

The other wall was taken up by a bow-fronted glass cabinet on whose glass shelves self-consciously rather than self-confidently sat their best china, consisting of half a dozen cups, saucers and small plates, a few odd sherry glasses and tumblers, a variety of unremarkable and kitsch figurines from day trips and longer summer holidays abroad together with his father's sole wartime booty: a delicately decorated coffee set of Meißen-stamped porcelain picked up at the end of the war during a warship's courtesy call in Schleswig Holstein. To compound his father's material misfortune, one of the cups and the sugar bowl belonging to this collection had been broken and badly glued together. Next to it stood a three-shelved bookcase stacked with two sets of encyclopaedias and a selection of fiction and non-fiction books, none of them classics, except Scott's *Waverley* novels. An assortment of enlarged, mounted and framed photographs sat on top of both items of furniture.

The three of them would chat about current affairs and he would give his mother a smidgen of his London gossip for nourishment. This mainly consisted of the life and times of those of his friends whom she had met or whose names she at least knew. Tony thought of past occasions when he had perversely withheld information from them or deliberately denied them an anecdote originating in his universe that they would have doubly enjoyed if he had shared it with them. In fact, rather cruelly, should he sense that he was overfeeding their appetite for news about his life, he would pre-emptively declare, 'Time to go for a stroll' – which served as a prompt for one of them to say as he closed the sitting room door and went down the stairs, 'Don't forget your key, son.'

This alienation of parent and child witnessed in the

unwillingness of children to allow their parents to peer as observers through the stained glass window into their lives is deepened by the fact that not only do children regard the pasts of their begetters as too dull to merit exploration, but they also consider that they have little or nothing to gain from their knowledge and experience.

So, while parents are eager to know about the lives of their children, the latter rarely have much interest in the lives of their parents until it is too late; they are too full of their own lives and times.

Just as an episode of the serial that they watched each Friday evening came to an end, his mother's earlier words began to ring in his ears like a reminder bell. He glanced up at the mantelpiece at the centre of which, set in a frame of mock mahogany, was the Roman face of a loudly ticking clock. He stood up and said, 'Time to go and stretch my legs. Do you fancy coming, Dad?'

'That's a good idea, Tony, get your old dad out of the house,' his mother quickly chipped in.

'Oh, alright. Perhaps I shall then,' his father slowly replied putting down the newspaper that he had been unfolding.

It was the word 'then' that captured the spirit of his father's unvoiced, internal soliloquy; Tony surmised that by inserting this little word into his sentence his father wanted to suggest that his decision on whether or not to accept his son's hardly effusive invitation had not been a foregone conclusion. In fact, by hesitating he hoped to convey the message that his first reaction was to decline. However, 'then', he had retracted his initial (unspoken) rejection of the offer because of his son's insistence that he join him for a drink. Tony could not at that time in his own life imagine how pleased and proud his father was to join his son in going for a drink.

Rather than hoof it to his usual haunts that were peppered around the harbour, when Tony and his father left the house they turned up the hill and went across the park, skirted around the defunct bandstand, down a well-lit, car-free lane and walked through the Double Diamond-initialled, frosted-glass-panelled door into the forlorn saloon bar of a respectable, quiet commercial hotel. As it was Friday night its normal clientele of travelling salesmen had gone home for the weekend, allowing local residents to claim possession: an elderly couple out for their weekly drink sat in one corner, quietly ruminating and sipping their respective glasses of Babycham and Worthington; a middle-aged foursome had taken over a larger table in the centre of the room and were chatting and joking animatedly, while two young, adult males escaping their families for the evening were perched on bar stools savouring every minute of their boys-alone banter.

Tony steered his father towards a corner seat out of hearing distance of the other customers. Seeing that the legs of one of the chairs were wobbly he searched around and brought back a comfortable Parker Knoll. 'There you are, Dad. Now what can I get for you?'

'A small Mackeson, please, son.'

'Are you really sure about that?'

'No. Alright, I'll have a half Double Diamond instead.'

Tony was glad that he'd changed his mind, for Mackeson was a brand of stout that held unpleasant memories for him. It had been the favourite tipple of his mother's younger brother who had lived with them, together with her elder brother and mother, until Tony had left home. Tony gave an involuntary sigh at the deeply unhappy memory triggered by his father's choice of Mackeson. It was this not much older, emotionally disturbed, bachelor uncle from whom he had received his hand-me-down clothes; he had also supplemented his pocket money into his mid-teens by allowing him to keep the money from the returns on his empty 'Mac' bottles when Tony took them to the off-licence and brought back replacements.

'Here's the money for two small Macs and you can keep the change on the bottles.' Tuppence a bottle. Six bottles times two. Nearly the price of a packet of five cigarettes. Woodbine produced a packet of five, or the shopkeeper split a packet of ten; so did Benson & Hedges whose tobacco tasted sweeter than the rough old 'woodies'; B & H were more like the light green 'Golden Virginia', or the honey rich, dark brown 'Old Holborn' roll-ups, which they puffed 'up on the Green' or in the youth club, which had been offered a place in the church hall.

This was the fifties and the new estate reflected the

Government's post-war socialist priorities. Families were allotted brand new council houses with front and back gardens and children had schools to go to. At first the primary school was also used as the venue for Anglican Church services on Sundays. The Methodists had already erected a chapel for their worshipers and the Jehovah's Witnesses had set up their stall in a Nissen hut. Then a man had come round knocking on the door asking residents whether they wanted a pub. One was built anyway, followed by another, across the Green next to the doctor's surgery. Soon afterwards the Church of England built its own modern hall to God without a public opinion survey.

It was so noisy in the council house, especially in the summer when the canned laughter and cowboy shoot-outs not only travelled up through the thin ceiling but out of the downstairs windows, into the garden and then barged their way back into the house through his upstairs bedsitting-room window. Tony remembered vividly his frustration at being unable to close his ears like a deaf monkey to what he did not want to hear and his reluctance to go downstairs again and ask his uncle, grandmother and mother to reduce the sound a little bit more.

He shut his eyes and saw himself close his school textbook, put it in a small holdall, and leave the house quietly through the front door. Because at the Mayflower, which sat like a dry-docked sloop at the top of the road, they knew that he was under age, he would traipse across the Green to the Bull and Bush where he could order.

While his uncles drank stouts he preferred light ale, with a dash of lime. It was in the gaudy carpeted lounge, at an empty table in an almost empty room, warmed by occasional chuckles and rarely disturbed by jukebox music, that he relaxed with Percy Bysshe. That too was then.

A couple of months after Tony had fled the nest, his mother had written to him to say that, following an argument with her younger brother, she and Dad had moved out of their extended family's council house into an unfurnished flat. It was to their new home, where the two of them were now for the first time living entirely alone away from her two siblings and unstable mother, that he returned for Christmas. He slept on a made-up couch in a narrow room – no more than a corridor with a bulge – through which his parents had to pass in order to reach the kitchen and outside lavatory. The flat, though large, had no bathroom. They had remained there for just eighteen months before moving to the flat where they now lived and which they rented from a retired naval officer.

'There you are, Dad,' he said settling the glass down on a beer mat and himself on the bench seat to face his father, with his back to the curtained window. 'And, I've bought you some crisps.'

'Cheers, my son,' the old man said as he raised his drink and reached with the other for the salt and vinegar flavoured Smith's. Tony looked at the old man's hands, one gripping the handle and the other stretched across the table. Disproportionately large in relation to the rest of his wiry, diminutive frame, his hands with their knotted fingers and knuckles and the thick-ridged, blue veins that ran across them would have attracted the attention of a Durer, da Vinci or Michelangelo who would have seen in them both an almost wincing unsightliness and at the same time a quintessential feature of humanity. The hands and weather-worn face were etched and sculpted by his long, mostly torturous, journey through European history beginning in the first decade of the twentieth century.

'So, what do you make of this latest political peccadillo, then, Dad?'

'It's same old story. Politicians never learn from the history. Rich, well-educated man but behave like know nothing.'

The branch of the Indo-European family of languages spoken in the place where his father was born did not use the definite or indefinite article. Tony could deal with that easily enough; much more difficult for him was his father's ungrammatical structuring of English sentences – verb tenses, placing of prepositions and reversal of compound words. It made a very literate man sound totally illiterate. When he spoke, Tony discerned how the sentence structure would have sounded perfectly correct in his native tongue; yet, in English, for most people, even those who knew and were very fond of him, trying to understand what he was saying could be quite exasperating. As a result, when in company, Tony had grown accustomed to taking on the role of interpreter, repeating what his father had said as he had intended the content to be understood.

'Shh. Don't speak so loudly, Dad,' he whispered.

His father looked around to see if anyone could hear him. No one of course could, even had they been interested in doing so. Tony was back in a familiar space, balancing his permanent feeling of embarrassment about his father with a deep affection for him. The interaction of these emotions kept alive a desire to find out more about his father's past. He had convinced himself that the more information he could amass about his father's life and what he had seen and endured, the better he would be able to understand the man. More than that, though, Tony believed that his father's story of his family and personal journey would provide him with a distinctive slant on the events that shaped the Continent's twentieth-century history.

'I wanted to ask you about the years running up to the war…' Tony continued.

His father seemed lost, not knowing where to begin, partly because he was not really sure what it was his son wanted to know. He would prefer to talk about current affairs not about his life since childhood. Least of all did he want to think about his first wife and the two children he had left behind. Not that this part of his life interested Tony, for he too had buried deep inside his brain's bunker the memory chip containing the little information that he had gleaned about a half brother and sister born before the war in another country.

Tony's eyes followed his father as he walked slowly but militarily upright to the lavatory, grimacing at the fact that his jacket was as ill-fitting as ever. Why did his mother, who took responsibility for choosing his clothes, always, always buy jackets and coats at least one size too large so that his hands barely protruded out of the sleeve – especially since she was so particular about ensuring that her dresses, skirts and coats fitted her perfectly? Was she still afraid, even at this late stage in their lives, that another elderly (possibly better-off) woman might find a dapperly dressed, strikingly polite gentleman, with a sense of humour and who enjoyed exercising his baritone voice, attractive enough to become a rival for his affections? Unlikely, Tony thought, but no doubt it was a fear that could be sparked off by what his mother might regard as over-attentive courteousness to another woman.

A more straightforward and at least equally probable explanation was her anxiety to conceal as far as possible her husband's discomforting hands. However, apart from its size, the jacket was fine; it was clean and not worn out. In any case, he grinned to himself as he scanned the bar, no one in the room, or anywhere else for that matter, took any notice of this grey-haired, bespectacled elderly gentleman.

Tony flinched again as another memory broke through his protective barrier as an admonishing spectre: he saw his father wearing his shabby working clothes and Wellington boots, not coming down the street, but at the school sports day where he, Tony, in his late teens, was competing in the 800 metres race, which he won. He remembered the sense of shame he felt at his father's appearance in his labourer's togs. His recall of the event was always unclear; he couldn't be really certain what his father had been wearing, whether he had come close to the track or hovered as a bystander further away, whether he, Tony, had gone up to him or ignored him. However, the detail of the occasion was less important than the kernel of the memory that remained: the very disquieting sense of shame that he had felt about his father's foreign name, the way he spoke and his worker's garb and occupation.

At that moment he felt wrapped up in and choked by layer after layer of shame and reproach for his father; he wasn't just ashamed of his father but also of his own background. These smothering emotions were finally gift-wrapped in tormenting guilt; how could he harbour such an abhorrent feeling as being ashamed of his father?

'Fancy one last one?' Tony asked.

'Oh, no. No thanks, my son. I've had two halves already.'

'I'll just have another half, before we go, if you don't mind.'

'You go ahead. I'm fine.'

They talked about the mundane and jumped from one political issue to another. Sadly for Tony, all those questions that he always wanted to pose to his father about his life had evaporated as soon as they took their first sips of beer. Still, father and son had chatted easily and time had passed quickly.

Tony returned their empty glasses to the bar and left just as the balding and moustached barman, who had evidently mastered the art of indolence, tucked away his weekly magazine under the counter and prepared to call time. Little was said by either father or son during their short stroll back through the park in the warm night air under a clear sky; the teeming questions that he wanted to ask sat dozing in his head until another occasion. As father led son up the stairs to the first floor flat his mother came out onto the landing, her hair in night curlers.

'There you are then, at last. I was beginning to get worried. Still, you must have enjoyed yourselves.'

'I'll help you make up your bed,' his father said, opening the sideboard and taking out the bedding.

'No, I'll do that. You two go to bed. I was thinking, why don't I take you out for a meal tomorrow?' Although he didn't find it a terribly appealing idea, he wanted to treat them.

'Not necessary,' his father said, curtly, as he invariably did when Tony made any suggestion which might entail his spending money on them.

'Dad's right. You can't afford to do things like that,' his mother echoed. Tony wavered, but knowing that they would both enjoy it, insisted that they go to the 'Roma in Bocca'. This was a relatively new Italian restaurant with a décor that he knew would appeal to them. To his surprise, for some reason it had not become fashionable, which together with the fact that it was mid-week meant that the restaurant was unlikely to be fully booked.

Nevertheless, to be on the safe side, he would go there during the day to select and reserve an appropriately situated table.

He bowed his head to be kissed by each parent in turn; they went to their room, he made up his bed on the couch. In the process he mentally prepared himself for a restless night in the full knowledge that the temporary discomfort was of no consequence at all; he had done his duty and in just another thirty-six hours he would be off again. He also knew that as soon as he had gone down the stairs, closed the door behind him, waved to them in the upstairs window, walked up the hill, turned the corner into the back lane, crossed the park to the station and sat down in his reserved seat on the train, that the words he could not find when he was with his father would condense again into questions – in fact, a whole interrogation sheet that would never be answered.

He raised his head from the book on which he had been trying to concentrate and looked out of the window of the TGV as it sped down the Rhone valley. He knew the countryside well and, looking at the vine-clad slopes, compared them with the landscape that as a schoolboy he had chugged through daily, sitting in a smoke-drenched pre-war carriage drawn by a stout, tanker-class, coal-fed engine. Half a century ago, the speed of the train had been slow, its compartment of velveteen bench seating for eight people elbow to elbow cosy and dirty; now, by contrast, the train was fast and its aircraft bucket-type seats detergent clean.

Although they met at least twice a year, their paths rarely crossed without careful planning. The last time their lives had intersected in time and space in an unplanned manner had occurred many years ago when they both happened to be in Weimar at the same time. On that occasion they had visited the nearby Buchenwald concentration camp together, where 55,000 people, at the very minimum, had perished. What they had seen, as much as what they learned from the permanent exhibition about the camp, from its initial construction in 1934 to its liberation in 1945, left an everlasting impression on both their lives. This time, they discovered that they would be in Grenoble at the same time but attending different events.

As soon as the dates were fully confirmed she had immediately checked to see whether the theme of this year's annual exhibition would be of interest to them. Fortuitously, the theme, 'Depictions of Wintry Scenes from the 16th to the 18th Century', which included paintings by Pieter Bruegel the Elder and the Younger, appealed to both of them. Since their post-show discussion of the exhibition and its curation had been interrupted, they agreed that they should continue their conversation on the train in which they would be travelling together the next day.

★

'Hello, dear, I thought that you had left me,' he said smiling at the young woman who sat down at the table opposite him.

'No. Why would I do a thing like that, Dad? I needed to make a couple of phone calls.'

'Friends or work? Anyone I might know?'

'Work, unfortunately. And, no. It was no one you know or would even want to be associated with,' she said.

'I was just thinking about that exhibition,' he said.

'That's strange, so was I,' she laughed with an exclamation mark.

'Which ones did you like best?' he asked.

'Well, it's difficult not to be impressed and fascinated by all of the Bruegels' paintings. It's a pity so many are in private collections and never seen by a broader public. Of the ones on display, my favourites were the *Wintry Landscape*, *The Hunters in the Snow* and, despite the subject and its title, *The Massacre of the Innocents*,' she said.

'I agree with your first two choices, but I'm not so sure about your third.'

'It helps to keep my mind focused,' she said turning to look out of the window.

'I know what you mean,' Tony said nodding his head. But then to lighten the subject said jokingly, 'It's interesting that you chose three paintings by Bruegel the Elder.'

'No, I didn't. Only *The Hunters in the Snow* was by the Elder,' she said slightly tentatively for, although confident that she was correct, she was disinclined to assert her authority on the subject.

'My mistake. I'm sure you're right,' he conceded, just as his father had invariably done with him when he was the same age and they disagreed.

Arguing is rarely worthwhile and it never is between parents and grown-up children. Without a further word being spoken father and daughter consented to hold to their own opinions. It was she who switched tracks and took them across more peaceful terrain.

'I also phoned your granddaughter, the responsible one in the family, to make sure everything's ready at home for your extended weekend and that there's a bottle of your favourite Mâcon in the fridge.'

'Just one bottle?' he asked mischievously.

'Of course, at least one. Now tell me about your birthday. I'm very sorry that I couldn't celebrate it with you. It was your eightieth after all.'

'That's alright. I know what a busy life you lead. And, to be honest, I never thought I'd make it this far.'

'Oh, come off it, Dad. You always used to say that you wanted to live one year more than Grandpa. Which means that you've another five to go.'

'I know that that's what I said, but he didn't abuse his body. Do you remember how he used to say, "Some people live to eat but I eat to live"? That sums up so much about him and his generation. I grew up in different circumstances,' he sighed and looked at his daughter. 'Unlike him I've abused my body too much and as I grew up I relished the idea of becoming a *bon vivant*, and unlike him decided I wanted to live in order to eat. And, of course, drink.' He leant across the table and, touching her hand, gave a broad, happy grin.

He pulled the sheet up higher and turned over. He felt no pain. The National Health Service with which he had grown from boy to man ensured that. This was part of the compact into which he had been born, midwifed by Mr Beveridge. The comprehensive Welfare State meant that he would not have to fear the valley of the shadow of death; everything would be taken care of. Not like the time in Istanbul many years ago when, with his stomach liquefying on the stroke of the quarter hour, he used his limited funds to admit himself to the German hospital, built, as had been his secondary school, during the Napoleonic Wars.

That ward had been palatial, the floor polished to the satisfaction of any Narcissus walking across it, the ceilings high and the wide windows open to let in the wail of the muezzin at dusk and dawn. Then, just as the sun set, a matronly nurse, a nun from the adjacent convent, whose attire was as starched as his sheets, began to play a harmonica as she swayed along the carbolic-clean corridors.

He shared the nurse's melancholic air with just one other patient, whose plastered leg was hoisted up as in a sitcom or postcard which playfully parodied anyone unfortunate enough to be hospitalised. They did not talk and no one visited, apart from a Lancastrian, working class, androgynous girl with an urchin cut. Chris wore a blue and white horizontally striped T-shirt and used her bra like a belt to flatten her flat chest further. As far as he was aware, he had been the last person whom she had invited to screw her. It had been kind of her to come to see him; she watched him sip his sweet tea and swallow cinnamon-flavoured crushed apple and gave him an Ian Fleming paperback. That too was a long time ago. Tears came at the memory, not of her, nor of the nurse, but of the time.

The shutter on the cord of the memory frame closed and he opened his eyes on the present. She was sitting there looking at him and as his eyes opened like a venetian blind, so did her mouth in a broad smile. He took her hand which lay on the sheet. Those memories were part of his story that she would never know.

'You didn't finish the Mâcon,' she said.

'I'll have it later,' he said giving her hand a soft squeeze. 'Not the same glass, I hope.'

'Definitely not. But don't worry, we always have a bottle in stock for you.'

'The journey's not over yet, is it?'

'No, Dad. You seemed only to have reached Istanbul. You've got years to go. Lots more travelling still to do, forwards as well as backwards, which I'd like you to tell me about, one day.'